Wayne Short

THIS RAW LAND

by Wayne Short

-Devil's Thumb Press-

THIS RAW LAND

Printing History

©Copyright 1968 by Wayne Short
All rights reserved under International and
Pan American conventions

Library of Congress Catalog number 68-14509

First printing by Random House, 1968, New York

One printing John Farquarson LTD, London, England

First Devil's Thumb Press Printing 1988

Second Devil's Thumb Press Printing 1995

Third Devil's Thumb Press Printing 2002

Other books by Wayne Short:

The Cheechakoes
This Raw Land
Albie, and Billy, the Sky Pilot & Other Stories
Luke Short, A Biography

ISBN 0-96744980-6-5

Cover by Walter Richards

This book is for my brother, Robert Neil (Dutch) Short, fishing, hunting, trapping companion, fireside philosopher when day was done—lost with his fishing vessel, **Anne II**, *one violent winter day somewhere between Five Finger Light and Midway Island, southeastern Alaska, February 24-25, 1966.*

FOREWORD

Along the North Pacific Coast between the 54th and the 60th parallels there stretches an awesome group of islands known as the Alexander Archipelago. From the outermost islands, east to the Canadian border, it is a mere 120 miles wide, and only 330 miles in length. It is commonly called the Alaskan Panhandle. It is a vast land, not in miles perhaps, but by reason of its utter remoteness. There are no roads, except for a few miles on each side of the small towns and villages which are scattered thinly on the islands and mainland shore. To travel one must go either by boat or airplane.

Within its boundaries are more than 7,000 islands, ranging in size from small rocky islets with their stunted windblown trees to some that are over 100 miles in length. There are straits and sounds and deep passages separating the islands, and bay and inlets so numerous that a man could spend a lifetime and still not explore them all. Mountains rise from the water to majestic snow-capped peaks high in the sky; mountains with age-old glaciers relentlessly creeping down between them to be devoured eventually by the persistent sea; mountains stretch endlessly away into the interior.

Wildlife abounds here: deer, black bear, brown bear, grizzlies, mountain goats, as well as moose up the mainland river valleys. Countless seals and sea lions, whales, killer whales, and porpoise feed and live in the inland waterways. It is a fisherman's and bird hunter's paradise.

— FOREWORD —

This is a land of strange contrasts. It can be lonely, as a loon's demented laugh floats across an isolated bay; sometimes it is breath-takingly beautiful; and it can be a violent land, too, just waiting to catch you at a weak moment and kill you.

Into this raw land I brought my young wife—and this is the story of the life we made there.

Wayne Short

Warm Springs Bay
Baranof, Alaska

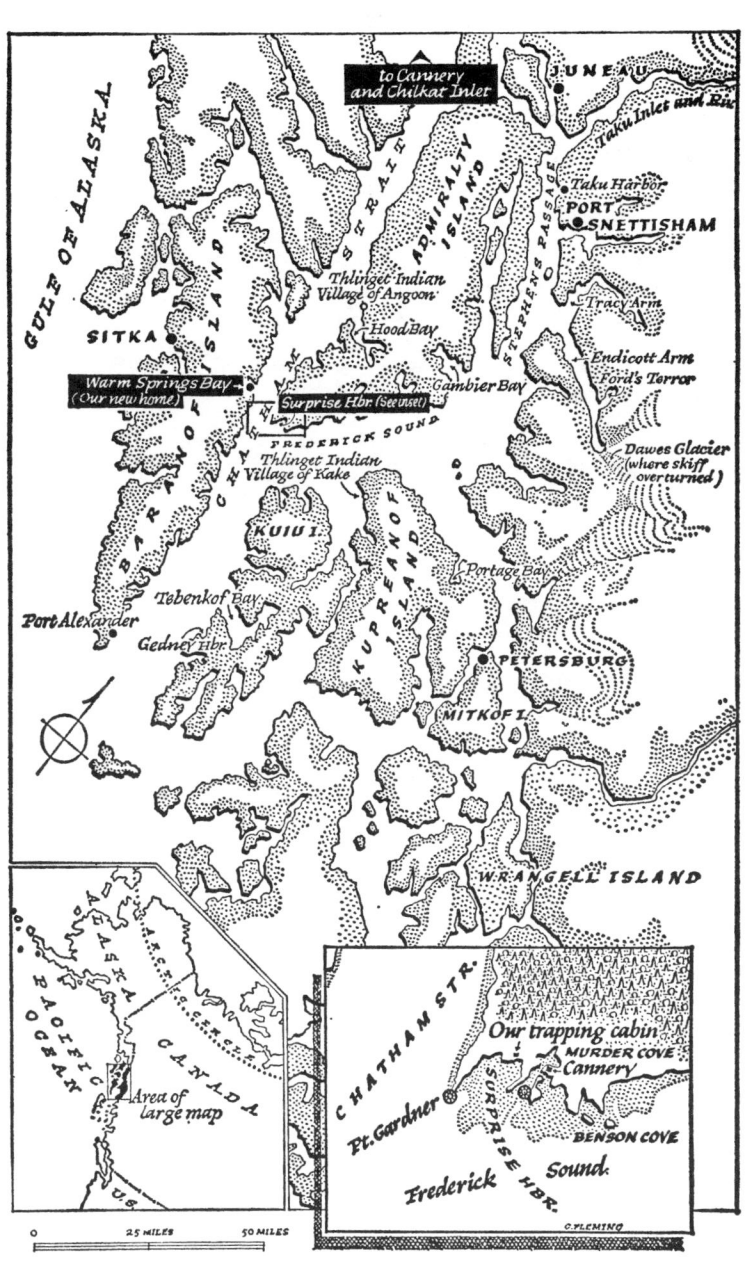

CONTENTS

Foreword ix

PART ONE:

1—*The Bride* 3
2—*Whales and Killer Whales* 11
3—*Halibut Fishermen* 22
4—*King Salmon* 31
5—*Fur Seal and Sea Lion* 40
6—*Coho Fishermen* 49

PART TWO:

7—*Deer and Brown Bear* 57
8—*The Trappers* 68
9—*Christmas* 79
10—*Sea Voyage* 86
11—*Ordeal* 96
12—*The Frontier Wife* 113

PART THREE:

13—*The Fish Buyers* 119
14—*Salmon Run!* 134
15—*A Night to Remember* 141
16—*End of the Season* 150

PART FOUR:

17—*Murder Cove* 159
18—*Bear, Behind You!* 176
19—*The Lonely Land* 184
20—*Dangerous Dan Willis* 189
21—*The Changing Land* 195

PART ONE

1

The Bride

At five-thirty we awoke to loud explosions outside our door. "What on earth is that?" Barb asked, sitting bolt-upright in bed.

"Just Duke shooting the shotgun to wake us up for breakfast," I said, and began to get up.

"Does he do that *every* morning?" she asked.

I laughed, and went into the bathroom and climbed into the big wooden bathtub full of hot mineral water. I soaked luxuriously for twenty minutes, then dried off and dressed. My bride of forty-eight hours had gone back to sleep. I lifted the covers and smacked her sharply across the fanny with the flat of my hand. "Daylight in the swamp, *cheechako!*" I yelled. "Hit the deck! The honeymoon is over and we have a boat to get ready to fish." She rolled over, groaned, and sat up rubbing her eyes.

I left her and stepped outside to the boardwalk. Already the sun was trying to muscle its way over the mountains in the east. The crisp Alaskan sea air still had the breath of winter in it, and after having spent seven months breathing industrial smoke and automobile fumes in San Francisco, I thought it tasted mighty good. I propped a foot on the boardwalk railing and lit a cigar. In this early-morning stillness a multitude of sounds came: the chirp of a land otter over near the falls; presently I heard the hysterical laugh of a loon; then out near the entrance of the bay a whale blew as it fed on herring, and the sun touched its spout of vapor. A bald eagle shrieked from the top of a tall spruce nearby, then all was quiet for a moment. It was good to be home again.

I stood there smoking and savoring the goodness of this moment, thinking back to the beginning, pondering the often unrelated little incidents that sometimes have such a profound effect on a man's life. . . .

My father, whom we all call Pap, is a small, wiry man who, until we moved to Alaska, had never stayed in one spot or on the same job long enough to leave more than a trace of himself. Not that there was anything shiftless or lazy about Pap; on the contrary, he was a hustler of the first order. He just wanted to be his own man, in his own way. Pap quit his first good job, a position with Standard Oil Company, two years before I was born, because his immediate superior suggested that in the future he should wear a white shirt and tie to work. "To hell with that kind of outfit!" Pap said, to my mother's dismay. "We'll move out to the Arizona desert and homestead"—and they did. I was born there, and in the next twenty years our trail wandered back and forth across the western states like the mark of a snake in the throes of violent death.

The Bride

Robert Service, in one of his poems, wrote: *There's men that just don't fit in* . . . that was Pap, avoiding modern-day regimentation like a plague. And I'm afraid my two younger brothers and I were cast from the same mold.

On a rainy spring night in 1946, we stepped off the steamer *North Sea* in the little frontier fishing community of Petersburg, Alaska, and, with my long-suffering mother looking wistfully back at the scattered houses of the settlement, set out in our little twenty-two-foot surplus lifeboat to carve a home and livelihood from the wilderness. We had established ourselves and, *cheechakoes* that we were, had learned to survive the hard way.

Now, eight years later, I had just returned from a winter in San Francisco, where Barbara and I had been married. She was a city-bred girl from Sioux City, Iowa, and had been working as a registered nurse in a San Francisco hospital when I met her and brought her back to share our lonely life in the Alaskan bush. Last night, my brother Duke had said to her: "When the new wears off and the boredom sets in—you'll leave. I'll give you a year at the most."

Barb had answered: "I'll be here a year from now, smarty—and twenty years from now! How'd you like to make a little bet?"

The door of our cabin suddenly opened behind me and Barb stepped outside, slim and straight, looking like a million dollars.

"What are you doing?" she asked with a smile.

"Just thinking," I said, taking her hand, and we began walking down the boardwalk toward Ma's for breakfast.

Ma is innately shy, and after spending thirty years

following Pap's wandering footsteps and living in lonely, isolated spots, finds it hard to make small talk with strangers. As Ma served breakfast, she was ill-at-ease with Barb. I could tell from the expression on her face that although she would welcome another woman's company, she did not really think that a young woman from the city would be content to live our isolated life.

My two brothers, Duke and Dutch, six-footers both, affecting heavy mustaches, were putting grub away like they could see a famine coming. Barb watched them in amazement, then said to Ma, "This sausage is delicious."

"Pap makes it," I said. "It's one of his specialties—making sausage, sugar-curing venison hams, and smoking salmon."

"How do you do it, Pap?" Barb asked.

Pap told her how he ordered pork side meat from town on the mailboat, ground and mixed it with venison, then seasoned it. I got up to get the coffeepot from the stove, and Ma said in a low voice: "What will Barbara think of us—of the way we live?"

"What's wrong with the way we live, Ma?" I asked.

Ma waved a hand. "The furniture, the . . ."

"She probably thinks it's quaint and frontierish. You know something, Ma, people down in the States go for all that now."

"Go for what?"

"Well, for instance, people will pay twice as much for old, weathered, used bricks for their fireplace than they would have to pay for brand-new ones."

"Why?"

I shrugged. "It's just fashionable to have a lot of old stuff around. Probably we could peddle that hand-

The Bride

hewed, yellow cedar easy chair of yours down there and make enough to outfit the whole house with new furniture!"

"Do you think Barbara will . . ."

"Don't worry about her, Ma, she's going to be all right."

When I got back to the table, my brothers were hurrahing Barb, feeling her out, seeing how easily they could rough her up. Pap, old southern gentleman that he is, was defending her.

After breakfast I showed Barb around the place. Warm Springs Bay, located on the eastern shore of Baranof Island, was now a ghost town, but in the early days it had been a thriving community with two general stores, a bakery, a laundry, several saloons, a sawmill, a fish saltry, as well as a house of ill fame. In the late twenties, the sawmill shut down, then the saltry, and people began moving away. In the years that followed, it served as a haven for commercial fishermen who wished to stop in for a hot mineral bath in the public bathhouses, and during prohibition as a bootleggers' hangout.

The previous year my family and I had bought the one remaining business in Warm Springs Bay. This consisted of a small general store, liquor store, bathhouse, as well as several furnished cabins for rent during the summer months. We had not bought it as a business opportunity, but as a nice place to live. There were several hot mineral springs on the mountain in back of the settlement and the water came down in a big wooden pipe and was piped into all the cabins. Our cold-water pipe line came from Baranof Lake with sufficient pressure to turn a small hydroelectric plant. The plant ran continuously and cost us about seven dollars a year to operate—the price of a new pair of V-belts and a little lube oil for the bearings.

Although commercial fishermen stopped in during the summer months, the winters were just as isolated as our original homesite in Surprise Harbor on Admiralty Island, for we were one hundred sea miles from Juneau and Sitka; Petersburg, the nearest town, was a good eighty miles to the east.

Pap, Dutch and I operated our own commercial fishing vessels during the summers, and Duke skippered a tender for a salmon cannery. We had persuaded Ma to operate the business during the summer months when we were out on the fishing grounds, and she had shown rare talent in her dealings with the commercial fishermen and local Indians who stopped in.

The following day Barb and I began working on my boat, getting it in shape to go fishing. It was a thirty-foot, V-bottomed troller with a shovel-like bow that had prompted other fishermen to dub it *Wooden Shoe*. The *Shoe*'s cabin and hull had to be scraped and painted, and this chore took Barb and me two full days. Ma, from the vantage point of her kitchen window, watched as Barb, clad in paint-smeared jeans, wielded a brush. "Well, she's not afraid of work," Ma said.

The following day we put the *Shoe* on the grid to copper paint the bottom. The grid is a series of twelve-by-twelve timbers bolted on the bottoms of driven piling on the beach. To put a boat on the grid, you simply run the boat up to the piling at high tide, and tie up. As the

The Bride

tide ebbs, the vessel gradually drops until it is sitting on the grid timbers, held upright by the piling. The fact that our tides sometimes reach a height of twenty-one feet amazed Barb. I explained some of the advantages and disadvantages of the big tides. Being able to put a vessel on a grid for repairs was one advantage; in areas where tides were small, this could not be done, and vessel owners had to pay to be hauled up on a marine ways. If you ran your vessel aground with the tide flooding, in most cases the incoming waters would raise you enough to free your vessel, but if the tide was ebbing when you went aground, your vessel might lay over so far when the tide went out that instead of raising, it would fill with water and sink when the tide began flooding again. All this was confusing to Barb, as was copper painting the *Shoe*'s bottom.

"Why all this work?" she asked.

"The poisonous copper elements in antifouling paint kill the wood bugs and worms that would otherwise eat up a wooden hull in a very short time," I explained.

"What bugs? And what sort of worms?"

So as we waited for the tide to go out and leave the *Wooden Shoe* high and dry upon the grid, I took Barb down on the beach until I found a stick of driftwood with part of the surface eaten away by small wood bugs. I showed her piling that had not been creosoted and were eaten almost in two. Farther along I found a drift log that had been sawed in half. On the face of the cut were round black holes the size of my forefingers. "Toredo holes," I said. "They're small sea worms that bore their way into untreated, underwater woods, leaving an entrance hole so small it is unnoticed. They have sharp teeth and bore a rotary hole as they move back and forth in the wood, growing and leaving their waste in the tunnels behind them."

"Oh." Barb said. "So that's why you copper paint every spring."

A week later the *Shoe* was ready to fish; the gasoline engine had been tuned up, new stainless steel trolling wire wound onto the gurdies, our bedding and clothing was aboard, the lockers were filled with groceries—and we were ready to go fishing.

Pap and Dutch had already left for the fishing grounds, and we were anxious to join them. A day came when we started the engine, said good-by to Ma, and steamed out the mouth of Warm Springs Bay into Chatham Strait.

2

Whales and Killer Whales

Our destination was Tyee on the southern tip of Admiralty Island. Tyee was the site of a salmon cannery and cold-storage plant which operated during the summer fishing season. The company, in addition to their canned-salmon operation, bought halibut and troll-caught king and coho salmon which were frozen and shipped to the States for the fresh-fish market. King salmon were also split and mild cured in huge thousand-pound barrels of brine, most of which were ultimately shipped to New York to be smoked.

Now, in May, the fleet of trollers were gathering to troll for halibut, and we would join them for a month until the king salmon began to show in sufficient quantities in June.

The day was clear, and behind us to the west Baranof Island thrust its snow-clad spires high into the blue sky.

"It's beautiful!" Barb exclaimed, and I nodded assent. "Does the snow ever melt from the peaks?"

"They get a little bare in late summer," I said, "but some of the valleys between the peaks are glacial." I handed the binoculars to her and pointed to the blue face of an ice mass between two majestic sentinels. "There are spots in Hoggatt and Gut Bays farther on down the shore where snow slides down off the mountains and piles up on the beach so deep it lasts the year around." I told her about the place in Hoggatt Bay where we sometimes tied our boats to the face of the snowslide and filled the holds with snow ice when we ran short of ice for our fish.

Ahead I saw several flashes of spray in the calm sea. "Porpoise," I said, pointing, "just watch, they'll turn and come to meet us."

And here they came, six of them on a beeline for the boat at full speed, their backs breaking the smooth surface of the sea like bullets fired from an automatic rifle. A moment later they bracketed the boat, crisscrossing beneath the bow at high speed, seeming to miss the hull and bow stem by fractions of an inch as they wheeled and cavorted and came back for another pass. Barb, fascinated by the playful creatures, went out onto the foredeck and watched them flash by at their breakneck clip.

As we neared Point Gardner we began to see herring in large patches flipping on the surface, and presently a large humpback whale surfaced and blew directly ahead of the boat, its immense tail outlined against the dark-green sea as it leisurely fed on herring. I eased the throttle off and put the clutch into neutral.

Whales and Killer Whales

We drifted and watched for the whale to reappear, for, like the porpoise, it was the first one Barb had ever seen. At last the whale broke surface a scant eighty yards from the boat with a great *whoosh,* sending up a column of steam as its hot breath hit the colder air.

"Phew!" Barb said, holding her nose, as the whale's vile breath of half-digested herring drifted our way.

Then as we waited for the humpback to blow again, an age-old drama suddenly took place before our startled eyes. A flotilla of killer whales moved silently in on the feeding leviathan, their great dorsal fins seeming to float like small boat sails upon the placid sea. Suddenly the humpback sensed the danger; his mammoth tail hit the surface of the water with the sound of a stick of dynamite going off, and he made for deeper water with a mighty blast from his blowhole that sounded like a cry of anguish.

The killers, like a well-coordinated team, were there ahead of him. He turned to go around them, but four new ones sailed in to slash and force him back toward shallower water. He dove, and they went after him. Now we saw blood in the swirling waters where they had been. They had the humpback now; it was only a matter of time until they killed him.

"What are they?" Barb asked breathlessly.

"Blackfish . . . killer whales," I said. "They'll head him into shallow water where he can't dive deep and get away, and they'll bite chunks out of him and wear him down until he's nearly dead, then tear away his lips and eat his tongue while he's still alive—it's a delicacy for them."

Barb shuddered. "It's ghastly."

I nodded. "I've only seen it once before—years ago."

Ahead, the killers were relentlessly herding the doomed humpback into the shallower waters of Surprise Harbor. Once we counted sixteen dorsal fins slicing through the water. Every now and then the frantic humpback would leap clear of the wolf pack, suspended for a brief fraction of a second in the air before crashing back into the sea with a thunderous sound that could be heard for miles.

For two hours we slowly followed the one-sided duel which could only end in death for the poor humpback whale. Finally the pack of killers wore him down and drove him toward the beach and systematically slashed him to death. I put the boat into gear and turned away as the bald eagles and ravens and crows on shore began to converge upon the unexpected feast the killer whales had deposited upon their doorstep; tonight the mink and otters and weasels would join the party, and tomorrow, perhaps a brown bear back in the brush would lift his snout into the breeze and amble down to drive all the others away while he gorged on the mountainous pile of rich blubber. . . .

It was midafternoon before we nosed our way in toward the small boat float in Murder Cove, where perhaps thirty fishing vessels were anchored in the harbor or tied to the float that was connected to the cold-storage dock. Boats were busy unloading their halibut catch at the cold-storage hoist. I slowed down and eased the *Wooden Shoe* in toward the float, Barb on the bow with a tie-up line in her hand.

As I pulled alongside the *Sea Hog* and backed down, a great bear of a man squeezed out of the tiny pilothouse and took Barb's line. We made the lines fast, adjusting our tire fenders until we were satisfied. Then the giant stuck out a hand like a ham and said: "Good to see you again, Wayne. The Dutchman was telling me you had got yourself a cook in San Francisco."

"Barb," I said, "meet Steve Ervin."

Steve was a crack crane operator by trade, but he, like so many others, had been bitten by the fishing bug, and every summer brought his small thirty-two-foot troller to Alaska from Puget Sound to chase the elusive fish. He was also a good storyteller, and there was usually a crowd of fishermen around his boat listening to his yarns, while he stood back in his trolling cockpit making up fishing gear.

Barb went inside to begin supper, and Steve and I talked fishing. The boats had been averaging from seven hundred to fifteen hundred pounds of halibut a day, Steve said, and the cold storage was paying ten cents a pound for chicken and large, fifteen cents for whales, and seventeen cents for medium.

Barb stuck her head out the doorway to ask what *chickens* and *whales* were. I explained that a chicken halibut was six to twelve pounds, a medium, twelve to sixty pounds, a large, sixty to eighty, and whales were eighty pounds on up.

"How *big* do they get?" Barb asked.

"I guess five hundred or six hundred pounds is the record," Steve said.

"Wow!"

I then told her about the one Pap had landed several years before that weighed three hundred and sixty pounds and was nine feet long.

After supper we washed and dried the dishes, then

stepped across the *Sea Hog* onto the float. Fishing boats of every description were tied on either side of the float, no two alike except for the type of fishing gear used. I had told Barb something of the strong individuality of commercial fishermen. Something inherent in their make-up turned these men from the conventional life of nine-to-five jobs, the steady pay check and yearly vacation, as well as perhaps the most important objection: a superior they might have to answer to. These rugged individuals came from all walks of life: a former Boeing electrical engineer, a college professor, a mortician, an auto salesman, a baker—now all hopeless slaves to the capricious sea.

Then there was the old breed, some of whom were the few remaining survivors of bygone eras—the gold rush of 1898, and the days of the windjammers.

Ahead, Cracker-box Mac's derelict vessel lay with a starboard list. I introduced Barb to Mac, then we moved on to Dave Matelski's *Wanderlust*. The *Wanderlust* was something to behold; many years' accumulation of various articles of fishing gear and equipment littered the deck, the pilothouse, and living area in the fo'c'sle. But this didn't bother Dave in the least. "Well, hell," he'd sometimes say when things got too deep, "we're not going to take ol' *Wanderlust* to the fair, anyway!"

Amid the chaos on the back deck were his three children and a carcass of a black bear he had killed a few days before on Kuiu Island. I could see where Dave had whittled a few steaks from a haunch. Dave, bald, in his sixties, suffered from chronic arthritis and usually had his twelve-year-old daughter Cindy or Davey, a couple of years younger, with him during the summer.

Whales and Killer Whales

The little one, Christian, was about two years old and dressed in diapers; she wore an old T-shirt of Dave's as a sort of gown. Dave, who lived in Wrangell, over a hundred miles to the southeast, explained that he and the kids had left home two weeks before to go out and fish for a few hours in front of the town. The day had been so nice, with the smell of spring in the air, that they had decided to prospect for fish and stay out a couple of days before going home. They had lost track of time, fishing one spot and then another, until finally they had decided to come to Tyee and fish halibut.

"But won't your wife be worried sick?" Barb asked anxiously.

"Oh, when we didn't come home, she probably figured we'd took off fishing somewhere," Dave said, unconcerned. "I'm going to drop her a letter, though, and let her know where we are."

As we talked, soot began to drift from the stovepipe of the *Wanderlust*'s oil cookstove and settle about us. Dave, telling Barb and me a story, brushed a flake from his bald head, then told his son to bring his *black* hat. Davey returned with the hat and Dave put it on; he wasn't going to let the falling soot interrupt his yarn.

When Barb and I walked up the ramp toward the cold storage and cannery, I told her that Dave had two hats—the black fedora for when the stove was sooting, and a cream-colored one for when it was not. Behind us we heard a fisherman yell: "For God's sake, Dave, turn that smoke machine down!"

Honest Jim, the fish buyer, was busy weighing up halibut as we stepped into the fishhouse. The floor was covered with the flat, white-bellied fish of every size: from barely legal six-pounders to one giant over two hundred pounds.

"They look just like those little flatfish you see in California markets with their eyes on top of their heads," Barb said.

"Flounders," I said.

While we stood talking to Honest Jim, George Pierce and his wife Frances walked in. George was the winter watchman who, when the cannery closed down and the crews returned to the States at the end of August, took care of the plant until the next spring. They were a young couple who had been married only two years before, and shortly afterward had come to Alaska to take this lonely, isolated job. During the summer season George worked in the powerhouse as one of the engineers.

I introduced them to Barb and we talked for a little before George said: "Let's walk on up to the house, Wayne. I have something you'll be interested in."

The cannery and cold storage were built upon piling; a wide boardwalk above the water led back onto the beach, where the powerhouse, company office, store, cookhouse and bunkhouses stood. We walked past the store building, where big-eyed Thlinget Indian children from the "row" (a string of small, red company cabins on the far side of the cannery) sipped cans of pop and watched us without expression.

George and Frances lived in a small house between the store and the mess hall; there was a high chicken-wire fence in front enclosing their lawn, and the fence was lined with men who worked in the cannery, as well as a sprinkling of Indians from the "row."

Whales and Killer Whales

"What are you holding," I asked George, "a bullfight?"

We found a place at the fence and saw a tiny brown bear standing on its hind legs and drinking pop from a can that Mike Goodman, the cannery superintendent, held. The little fellow had a circle of silver hair ringing his neck; he couldn't have been over eighteen inches tall.

"How'd you get him?" I asked.

"I looked out the back windows of the powerhouse one morning about ten days ago," George said, "and there he was, standing by himself in the tide grass. I looked around for the mother and didn't see her, so I put on a pair of heavy leather welding gloves and ran out and grabbed him real quick. Fierce little bugger, though," George said, showing me teeth marks on his forearm.

"Looks fairly tame now," I said.

"He's adapted pretty fast. Of course, the men have been bringing food over from the cookhouse and, as you see, he really goes for pop."

"What do you call him?" Barb asked.

"Jughead," George answered.

"What are you going to do with him, George?"

"Well, the zoo in Calgary, Canada, wants him, so I guess we'll ship him south on one of the company tenders when they go back to Seattle this fall, then by rail to Calgary."

"You realize what he'll weigh by fall?" I said.

George grinned. "I'd hate to guess—the way he's been eating."

(By early September, when George built a strong cage and wrestled Jughead aboard the *Fish Hawk*, he weighed approximately one hundred and sixty pounds, and was getting hard to control. In fact, only George and Bob Horchover, a young deck hand on one of the tenders, were able to get near Jughead without being roughed up.)

It was getting dusk, and Barb and I began walking back toward the dock. As we came abreast the superintendent's cottage, Baldy, Johnny Goodman's two-year-old eagle pet, blocked our way. Baldy, although he would not have the white head feathers of a bald eagle until he matured, had a vicious nature and would sometimes attack, usually sinking his beak and talons into your ankles if you weren't fast on your feet. Barb stepped behind me as Baldy cocked his head and gave us the eagle eye. I made a couple of feints, but Baldy quickly countered like a trained fencer. Finally, rather than battle him, we stepped off the boardwalk and made a detour. Baldy swiveled neatly around, watching malevolently with his beady eyes.

That night, as we lay in our bunks with only the gentle lapping of the sea against the hull to break the silence, there came a *chirp, chirp, chirp.*

"What kind of bird is that?" Barb asked.

"It's not a bird," I said, "it's a land otter swimming out in the bay." Then I began to tell her the Thlinget Indian legend of the Otter people and of the *kustakaw* who lured people away into the woods and changed them into otters.

"Don't say any more," Barb said, "first the killer whales eating the tongue out of that poor whale, then that nasty old eagle, now stories of witchcraft—"

Her words were broken by a long quavering laugh

from across the bay. A second later she was crawling into my bunk. "What was *that!*"

"Just a northern loon," I said, putting an arm around her.

"It sounds like an insane old lady," Barb said, shivering.

"You'll soon get used to hearing them," I said gently. A moment later the hysterical, demented laugh came again, then the birdlike chirp of the otter, closer this time. . . .

3

Halibut Fishermen

We were up next morning as the first faint streaks of red began to color the mainland mountains to the east. I started the engine and let the temperature come up while Barb made coffee. Other engines were starting in the clear morning air, and fishermen were untying their lines and moving out of Murder Cove toward the halibut grounds.

As soon as the engine was warmed up, we untied from the *Sea Hog* and moved out the channel. On a sandy beach on Walker Peninsula four Sitka black-tail deer stood silently, ears cocked forward, watching the stream of fishing vessels go by.

There were two areas where the trollers fished for halibut: One we called the flats, a fairly uniform bottom four miles long, that lay in twenty-five to forty fathoms of water between Yasha and Carol islands. This area was popular because the bottom was soft, and there was plenty of room to fish. The other area was located

Halibut Fishermen

midway between Point Gardner and Yasha Island, a small, soft-bottomed basin in thirty-two fathoms which was completely encircled by jagged, uneven rocks, pinnacles, and reefs that could strip off the leads and lines in short order, if one did not know the bottom intimately. This area we called the halibut hole, and it was preferred by those who knew it well. Although I had a fathometer on the boat, I had learned the treacherous boundaries of the hole years before by sounding it with a lead, and I used landmarks to fish it.

As we neared the hole I slowed down and moved back into the trolling cockpit, which was equipped with a steering wheel, clutch and throttle control. On the deck directly in front of me were the "gurdies," small bronze drums, complete with clutches and brakes, which were powered by a shaft turned by V-belts from the main engine. On each drum were one hundred fathoms of one-eighth-inch stainless steel wire. This wire went from the gurdy, through a block which hung from a davit on either side of the boat. On the end of the stainless steel line was attached a forty-five-pound lead, or "cannon ball" as they are commonly called. Starting just above the lead were two brass line markers which the leaders were snapped into, and which kept the leaders from sliding up and down the line. These line markers were crimped onto the line at regular intervals, so that as many leaders as desired could be added.

In trolling for salmon we used four lines which, after being lowered to the desired depths, were "tagged" onto the tips of the trolling poles (four spruce poles approximately thirty feet long that were lowered to forty-five-degree angles). In fishing for halibut, we did not use the trolling poles at all, but ran one line right over the side so I could hold onto it and feel the bottom, as well as the halibut when they hit it.

I put the lead over the side, and began snapping leaders between the line markers as I lowered the lead by using the brake on the gurdy. On the end of each leader was a "choked herring," a herring threaded on a hook with the leader half hitched around the mouth to give the herring the right action when being dragged through the water. When I had snapped on five or six leaders, I checked my landmarks to be sure I was on the edge of the "hole," lowered the lead until it touched bottom, then raised it up a couple of feet.

For this type of fishing, we trolled slowly into the current caused by the big inland tides, and this slows the boat down until the lures are moving very slowly across the soft-bottomed feeding grounds many fathoms below.

Halibut are enigmatic, as are most fish. Fishermen, marine biologists and oceanographers are learning more about them all the time, but there is still much we *don't* know. Halibut are basically bottom fish, feeding on herring, small fish, shrimp, crabs, squid and small octopi. For fish, as for most creatures, habitat regulates form. The halibut starts life looking similar to a pancake on edge, with an eye on each side and a mouth in front, in conventional fish form. As it grows, however, it becomes a horizontal pancake, with its bottom eye shifting to the top side of the head and its mouth twisting around toward the bottom. Thus it can grub in the sand or mud for shrimp or crabs, pursue small fish and at the same time keep a lookout for danger from above. Its white

Halibut Fishermen

belly is on the bottom, and the mottled greenish-brown of its topsides blends into the shade of the ocean bottom. No doubt it has the ability to change the color of its camouflaged skin when the bottom characteristics demand it. The halibut can be found in three hundred fathoms of water in the winter and early spring, and it can be found lurking in one or two fathoms in late summer. Unlike rock and sea bass, snappers and cods, halibut can also be brought from great depths without injury. Moreover, because of its great size, as well as the fact that it spends most of its time on the bottom, the halibut has few natural enemies, with the exception of man.

As we began trolling slowly along the soft bottom, I kept a hand on the stainless line; if the lead bumped bottom I put the gurdy clutch into gear and raised it a bit. Presently I felt a cautious nibbling or mouthing of the herring. I waited. At last a tremendous pull came; the halibut had been hooked. I called to Barb and had her come back and hold the line.

"It feels like a whopper!" she cried. "Hurry, pull it in!"

"We'll wait awhile," I said, "and maybe get one on each hook."

On either side of us fishermen were pulling halibut aboard, and presently I thrust the gurdy clutch in and began to bring our catch up. Barb, looking over the side, kept anxiously peering into the depths for a sight of the halibut; then we began to see white bellies flashing as they fought and twisted to free themselves. We had no fish on the top leader, but the other five each had one. I stopped the gurdy, pulled the first halibut in and hit it

— *THIS RAW LAND* —

on the top of the head with the backside of the gaff, then sunk the hook into its head and jerked it aboard. Then came the next, and the next. . . .

We fished all through the flood tide, and judging from the amount of halibut in the fish bins ahead of the gurdies, I guessed we had nearly one thousand pounds. As the tide began to swing, I got the lead hung up in the rocks forming the perimeter of the hole, and after trying to free it unsuccessfully, lost lead, line and leaders. We turned then and began to head for the harbor. I turned the helm over to Barb, and told her to follow the returning fishing boats while I began to butcher the halibut.

It was late afternoon by the time we slowly eased beneath the electric hoist at the fishhouse, and Honest Jim sent down an enormous metal bucket for our fish. When they were unloaded, we moved on to the float and tied up.

I shut the engine down and Barb and I walked up to the fishhouse to pick up our tickets. We had almost eleven hundred pounds—about $175 worth of fish.

"We're rich!" Barb exclaimed.

"It'll cost about fifty dollars to replace the gear we lost today," I said.

But there was no discouraging her. "We'll still have over a hundred dollars left . . . and tomorrow we'll make another one hundred and seventy-five more, and . . ."

During the night a thick blanket of fog rolled in, and when we awoke to the alarm clock at four-thirty, I could not see the cold-storage dock a hundred feet away. There would be no fishing today.

The fog was still thick the next day and I asked Barb

Halibut Fishermen

if she wanted to cross the peninsula separating Murder Cove from Surprise Harbor and look for the body of the humpback the killer whales had killed. I was sure it would be on the beach in Surprise Harbor. We lifted the dinghy from the top of the pilothouse and eased it into the water. Barb fixed a lunch while I put my .30–06 and a pair of binoculars into the skiff. We climbed in and I began rowing through the thick fog toward the far side of the bay.

We carried the light skiff above the high-tide mark, then stepped into the thick forest of spruce and hemlock and yellow cedar, moving single file along the trail that my family and I had used to cross the peninsula to the cabin we had built when we first came to Alaska back in 1946. I showed Barb the spot where a great brown bear had charged the family in 1947. Duke, in the lead, had fired four shots into the beast before it dropped at his feet.

A half hour later we crossed the peninsula and forded the small salmon stream from which we had carried water when we'd lived there. We passed the blackened ruins of our old cabin, then continued on along the beach toward Sign Bay.

"It's beautiful," Barb said, looking back toward the clearing where the house had been, "but it must have been terribly lonely for your mother."

"It was," I said, "but I don't think any of us realized it until much later."

Presently we came around a point of land, and there was the dead whale ahead on the beach. A swarm of eagles, ravens, crows and sea gulls circled around the carcass. A moment later I saw the cause of the disturbance: A large brown bear was guarding the whale. The whale carcass was perhaps two hundred yards away, and the industrious brownie hadn't winded us. We sat down and I took out the binoculars and focused them upon him. The bear was busily dragging a dead tree limb down the beach to the whale. While he'd been away all the birds had alighted; now he dropped the limb and routed them into the air again.

"What's it doing?" Barb whispered.

"Shhhh . . ." I said.

The brownie ignored the raucous cries of the birds and returned to grab the limb in its mouth, then dragged it down the beach across the dead whale's tail. Back it went to the drift at the high-tide line for another limb. I moved the binoculars back to the whale, studying it. The birds had lit once more and were pecking away until the bear returned and drove them off again. Only then did I realize what the brownie was attempting.

"Well, I'll be damned!" I said in wonder, and began laughing.

"What?"

Then I explained it to Barb. The bear was trying to cover up the whale!

My brothers and I often killed deer and cached them in the woods near the beach until we could come back with a skiff and outboard to pick them up. On rare occasions we would return to find that a brownie had eaten on our deer and covered what remained with brush. We learned that if we surprised the bear, in most cases we would have to kill him if we were determined to take the venison—for the brownie or grizzly will fight for what it considers his.

Halibut Fishermen

I handed the glasses to Barb and we continued to watch the frantic brownie dragging brush and limbs out of the woods in a vain attempt to cover the whale carcass. After watching awhile, I stood up, saying to Barb: "I'm going to see if he'll scare, so we can go up for a close look at the whale. You stay here."

"Oh, no you don't," Barb said. "Not without me!"

"All right," I said, "but stay several paces behind me." I jacked a shell into the chamber, slipped on the safety, and we started slowly across the sandy beach. The bear, still busy, hadn't noticed us.

"Ho, ho! You there, Mister Bear!" I yelled. "Move on!"

Around he swung, his big, ponderous body agile as a ballet dancer's. The hair of his hump began to rise, the malevolent little eyes locked onto us. I stopped. "Haw!" I yelled, and slapped the butt of the rifle with the flat of my hand. With a roar of rage, the bear wheeled and galloped up the beach, and we could see the brush shake with his passage. He made a brief half circle—and burst out running straight for us.

"This is it!" I said tightly to Barb, and flipped off the safety as the rifle came to shoulder. Steadying the gold bead of the front sight squarely upon the bear's broad chest, I waited. There were still eighty yards between us; I would have had time to put a couple of shots into the chest, and the others into the massive head. Suddenly he stopped with a shower of sand, glaring at us.

A brief moment passed and the brownie stood motionless, defying us.

"Turn around and *walk* back to the point," I said

softly to Barb, without taking my eyes off the bear. "I don't want to kill him, if I don't have to."

As soon as Barb was gone I began to back away, until we had reached the safety of the point.

"Whew!" she said, making a motion as if to wipe her brow.

I looked back across the beach; the bear still stood like a statue, daring us to come back. Presently he whirled and ran back to chase away the eagles, ravens, crows and gulls again.

"I guess we didn't want to see the whale, anyway," I said, flipping the rifle safety on.

"No," Barb said, "not if we have to fight *that* fellow!"

I slipped the rifle sling over my shoulder, then held out a hand in front of me. It was trembling ever so slightly. I grinned at my watching wife, and we began walking back the way we had come. . . .

The fog lifted the following day and we went back to halibut fishing. One day followed another; we continued to do well on the days we could fish, but we did lose some time to fog and storms. Before we knew it the month was gone, and with it, the halibut season. We headed the boat toward Warm Springs Bay to wash our clothes and take a real bath in a bathtub, and put on our salmon gear.

4

King Salmon

It is the fifth of June, and we are again fishing off Murder Cove. Four lines with leaders four fathoms apart sweep back from the tips of our trolling poles. We have a variety of lures out: spoons, plugs and several flashers. On a leader eighteen inches behind each flasher is a "fillet" of herring on a hook. The flasher not only catches a salmon's attention from a great distance, but also wobbles as it is dragged through the water and gives the fillet an enticing, swimming action.

We are trolling by ourselves along the Point Gardner shore, and have caught a couple of medium-sized king salmon. It is slow going. Out along the edge of the reef toward Yasha Island are several boats and fishermen, including my brother Dutch on the *Salty*, and Pap on the *Seal*. I have the radiophone on 2138 kilocycles, the boat band, and am listening to trollers crying the blues all over the country. They are always crying, even if they're in heavy fishing, for the simple reason that if they were to tell how good the fishing *really* was, competitors would swarm in from every point of the compass.

In recent years this crying has produced some immensely talented weepers. I think at the end of every season we should all get together and award Oscars for the best crying performances of the year. I turn up the volume on the radiophone and we listen to a typical conversation between two trollers:

"Yeah, well . . . that's about the way it looks here, George . . . no feed, no birds showing . . . nothing . . . never seen it so dead looking, by golly! Gonna have to make a move pretty quick . . . I've only got one little king about ten pounds . . . "

The other boat comes back and this troller's story is every bit as sad as the first one's:

" . . . well, I'm just working for the oil companies now—running around burning up a lot of fuel, and catching no fish. I don't know where to go . . ." The fisherman's voice fades away in despair.

"Doesn't sound so good for those boats," Barb says.

"You can't tell a thing by listening to them talk. They probably have a code worked out, and one might be telling the other that he's in the fish."

Dutch gives me a call, and I pick up the mike and answer. I tell him I have two salmon.

"Better come over here," he says briefly, and signs off.

I picture the puzzled looks on listeners' faces for a hundred miles away. *Where are they?* they think. And, *How good is it?*

I turn about in a loose circle to keep the lines from tangling, and increase the throttle setting as we head for the other boats.

King Salmon

As we sweep in along the reef I get herring at twenty fathoms on the fathometer. I go into the cockpit and lower the lines to thirty fathoms. Now I have the feed bracketed. Even before I have the last line down, one of the bow poles begins to bounce furiously.

"A big one!" I yell to Barb, who steps out on deck. Then one of the wing poles begins to work. "Ho! Ho!" I cry.

Joe Cash, on the *Flicka*, trolls by; he is fighting a big king. After he has landed the salmon, he holds up both hands, fingers wide-spaced.

"Joe's got ten kings," I tell Barb. The starboard bow pole that has been bouncing goes completely wild now; it acts like another big one has hit one of the lures. Barb is tense with excitement as I start to pull up the starboard main line. I unsnap the heavy-duty rubber snubber and coil the 120-pound test monofilament leaders on deck until I come to the bottom leader where the king is. The light twenty-pound lead sinker is stretched out from the side of the boat. I set the lead on deck and begin pulling in the twenty-foot leader hand over hand. The king suddenly slacks the line and runs under the boat. I quickly take up slack and try to guide the fish away from the boat's propeller. He comes up behind the boat now and breaks water. For the first time we see him—a big one. He runs to the side, and the line burns my fingers as the king stretches the leader out tight.

"Don't let him get away!" Barb cries.

He sulks at the end of the leader, the rubber snubber stretched out six feet. I ease him in and he runs under the boat again.

"The other bow pole is working like crazy!" Barb yells, but I have my hands too full with the fish to even look up. I ease the king up from the depths. I reach for my gaff, and as his nose breaks water, I hit him hard.

The thick body shudders, the tail works spasmodically; I stick the gaff hook into the king's head and jerk him aboard. He is a beauty that will dress out perhaps fifty pounds.

He has taken a herring-scale plug. I take the hook from his mouth and put the lures back out again.

We begin to run through herring flipping on the surface now. Herring gulls cry continuously, diving into the mass, fighting and gorging themselves, making up for the past winter when they soared over the empty sea searching for food. Cormorants and fish ducks of all kinds join in the feast. Hundreds of small sea snipe dot the surface as they feed on the amphipods that the herring are also eating. Even bald eagles from shore fly out and soar in just above the water and try to grab the wildly flipping herring while still in flight, but they are out of their element here.

Now all four poles are bouncing. I drink a steaming cup of coffee Barb has brought, then light a smoke and begin pulling fish once more. This is the kind of fishing a man dreams of. . . .

We had good fishing for a week; then the king salmon were suddenly and completely gone. The trollers began to fill their holds with ground ice at the cold storage in Murder Cove, and began to search for the salmon. Barb and I took ice one morning and ran up the Admiralty Island shore, stopping off Chapin Bay, where we caught a few salmon in the afternoon. We anchored that night in Chapin Bay—where the steep timbered

King Salmon

slopes rise overhead on both sides, making you feel like an ant in comparison. We saw several brown bear patrolling the beaches, one, a gigantic female with triplets cavorting ahead of her.

Even though it was now mid-June, the booming of the male grouse echoed far into the night as they sent out their love calls. Chapin Bay has always been one of my favorite anchorages.

At first light the next morning we were up. Barb made coffee while I brought the anchor aboard, and as we left I showed her a great natural arch in the rock of the mountain on the western shore. We went out the narrow entrance of the bay into Frederick Sound and continued up the shore, looking for "sign." Salmon will not stay where there is no feed, so you look for signs of herring, needle fish, candle fish, or small feed such as schools of young tom cod. The sea birds—the gulls, cormorants and various fish ducks—are your best indicators. The "feed" may be many fathoms deep and not show on the surface, but you may be sure that the birds will know it and be there waiting patiently for them to surface at slack tide or during the night. Gulls will be drifting aimlessly about or sitting on the rocky shore in their precise pecking order, the black, long-necked cormorants diving deep, keeping a sharp lookout for the schools of feed in the depths.

We passed Eliza Harbor, for it was barren of birds, and continued up the shore. Off Spruce Island we began to see the birds working; then I picked up a solid mass of feed at fifteen fathoms on the depth sounder. I slowed down and went back to put out the gear.

We began to catch a stray king occasionally, but

there did not seem to be a very big school of salmon here. Whales blew up ahead and the air was busy with birds working in the western entrance to Pybus Bay. I changed course and began trolling toward them.

Soon we were trolling through big schools of herring slipping on the surface, and humpback whales blew on each side of us. Barb, binoculars to her eyes, was fascinated, and just a little uncomfortable to be so close to them.

Generally whales stayed clear of boats, but a year or two before, a cannery tender had been cruising serenely among feeding whales in Icy Strait, when one had suddenly jumped completely over the bow of the vessel, taking off the foremast. The crew had been at a loss to explain the whale's actions. Surely, with its built-in sonar, the whale had known the vessel's position. It was possible that a pack of killer whales were pursuing the leviathan, although the crew had observed none.

Presently four humpback whales came to the surface with heads together. "Look at them!" I called to Barb. "See them working together and schooling the herring?" I steered the boat in a little nearer and we watched closely. Four gigantic heads broke the surface simultaneously, all moving slowly together, great mouths open, and in each mouth's center we could see the frantic boiling of herring. The giants' mouths closed, and slowly the four sank to swallow their mouthful of herring. This was real teamwork!

The humpback whale is found in all oceans, and in Alaska is common to the Bering Sea and the inland waters of southeastern Alaska. It has a thickset body and extremely long flippers. It is a great deal more active and

King Salmon

playful than any other species of whale, given to all kinds of surface acrobatics such as standing on its side and waving its enormous, barnacle-covered flippers in the air. Often it will leap completely clear of the water to land on its side with a thunderous splash. I once watched one leap into the air eighteen times in a row. The humpback is blackish in color, with mottled white underparts. The *baleen* is a springy, resilient material consisting of several hundred narrowly spaced blades which hang from the gums on each side of the mouth. They are frayed-like on the edges to form an effective screen for sifting out the tiny crustaceans on which the humpback also lives, in addition to herring when it is available.

I was busy explaining all this to Barb, when suddenly one of the bow poles bent almost double. Then the breaking strap snapped, which released the pole and put the stainless steel main line back on the davit. The boat listed hard to starboard, and the stainless steel wire began running out, slipping the brake band on the gurdy itself.

"What on earth—" Barb began.

At that moment a humpback surfaced on the other side of the boat, some sixty yards away. As the humpy rolled slowly and began to sound, I could see some of my lures hanging over the whale's enormous back like Christmas tree decorations. I waited, hoping the leaders would break and I'd get my main line back, but the wire was steadily unwinding from the gurdy drum, the brake band so hot it was smoking. Reluctantly I grabbed a pair of pliers and cut the line.

The humpy slowly surfaced again, farther away now. And if it was aware that a forty-five-pound lead, twenty fathoms of stainless steel wire, together with a wide assortment of lures were trailing, it gave no sign.

Barb, standing white-faced on deck, finally found her voice: "Let's get out of here before one of those monsters rams us!"

I had to agree that it might be a good idea, and began to pull the remaining gear aboard. As we were heading into Pybus Bay to anchor and mark and reel on more wire, I smiled and said, "Well, we didn't do *too* badly today; we've got about thirty dollars' worth of salmon— and only lost fifty dollars' worth of gear . . ."

But Barb, fixing lunch at the stove, did not even smile in return.

The humpback whales were still feeding the following morning when we went out again to fish. We gave them a wide berth, and trolled on out the channel without having a single salmon strike. There was plenty of feed, but evidently no salmon about. At noon we still didn't have a fish aboard, and I picked up our lines and we ran on up the shore to Brothers Islands, where we found the fish again. By evening we had twenty good-sized kings and went into Last Chance Harbor to anchor for the night.

For the next five days we had good fishing, without another boat in sight. I had called Dutch and Pap on the radiophone, telling them in our code that we were in fish, but they had gone prospecting down Chatham Strait and found equally good fishing off Patterson Bay.

Stephens Passage is known and hated by boatmen as an iceberg area. The faces of the many glaciers on the mainland shore are continually breaking off into bergs which, once lost to the persistent sea, drift out into the

King Salmon

passage, sometimes by the hundreds. The tricks of wind and tide carry them all over the passage, and running a small vessel at night in this area is extremely hazardous.

One morning Barb and I went out to fish and found icebergs for as far as the eye could see. They came in every size and description, sculptured by the elements into the weirdest shapes imaginable.

"Look at that one!" Barb demanded, pointing to a berg which looked like a huge Buddha, sitting placidly upon the sea with arms akimbo. We trolled on by, and when we looked back at it from another angle it appeared to be only an undistinguished chunk of age-old ice.

Later I took out the .30–06 and with three shots dropped an overhanging piece of ice into the sea. We then came in close and wrestled it aboard to fill our ice chest.

We rose to find that the salmon had vanished one morning, and ran back to sell our week's catch to the cold storage in Murder Cove.

5

Fur Seal and Sea Lion

A week later we had joined Pap and Dutch, who were fishing off Cape Ommaney on the southernmost tip of Baranof Island. This was much different country, for we were fishing the open sea here. Usually there was a big, long ocean swell running, and the action of the boat was completely different from that of the inside waters. Barb did not get seasick, but until she became used to the motion, she was uneasy and was revolted by the mere thought of food.

We fished out of Port Alexander, on the inland side of the cape, a ghost town that years before had been a major fishing community. Not only had it had a large trolling fleet, but the herring reduction plants in nearby Port Conclusion, Port Armstrong and Big Port Walter had added greatly to its economy. It had boasted at one time several hotels, restaurants, liquor stores and saloons, a bakery, post office, cold storage, public school, as well as a popular bordello operated by an unusual madam. She

Fur Seal and Sea Lion

employed a talented French chef whose culinary art was without equal, or so the fishermen said, as well as comely girls of the highest class.

Now the once-elegant buildings of a bygone era were neglected and weathered, standing there, it seemed, as if patiently waiting for the return of the "good old days."

There were less than a dozen permanent residents, most of whom were old-timers. Octogenarians like Bert Olson and Adam Wilson, remnants of the forgotten sailing-ship era, still fished during the summer months, recalling the days when they had rowed out in a skiff without all of our modern fishing equipment and swamp loaded their skiffs with king salmon in a few short hours.

One day as we trolled off Wooden Island a strange animal suddenly bobbed its head out of the sea a few yards from the side of the boat and studied me curiously. It took a long moment for me to identify the animal. It was a fur seal.

These friendly, playful animals once numbered in the millions, but the discovery of the Pribilof Islands (which had been hidden in the eternal fog for the previous thirty years) in 1786 touched off a wholesale slaughter of fur seals that was only equaled by the carnage of the American buffalo which preceded the settlement of the West.

The pelts of fur seal and sea otter were soon in great demand by wealthy Chinese, and then became fashionable in Europe, commanding outrageous prices.

The sealers' methods of obtaining the pelts (clubbing the defenseless animals to death by the thousands on the beaches) must have been sickening, but the sealers were as tough and bloodthirsty a breed as ever sailed the sea—and there was an enormous profit to be made. One company shipped 458,000 pelts in a ten-year period.

Consequently the fur seals were almost extinct by the time laws were passed to protect them. Now, under government control, they have been increasing in number for years. Present-day figures of the summer fur seal population on the Pribilofs is estimated well in excess of two million! The fur seal, however, is rarely seen in the inland waters of the Alexander Archipelago.

I called Barb out to see the friendly little animal, evidently a female, judging by its small size. I had never observed a fur seal at such close range. It showed absolutely no fear of us, diving and twisting and cavorting beneath the clear water on either side of us; then it would suddenly pop its sleek head up a few scant yards from the side of the boat and study us with big, friendly dark eyes. The little spike-like external ears and its soft grayish-brown fur distinguish it from the familiar hair seal. A moment later it would dive and we could follow every move beneath the water as it showed off for us, its every action a demonstration of maneuverability and celerity.

Dutch, who always carried his sixteen-millimeter Bolex movie camera with him, was trolling ahead about a mile. I called him on the radiophone and told him about the fur seal, still playing alongside us. Dutch turned his boat about and trolled back until we met, then eased in between us and the seal—and presently the friendly animal was following him!

It was a bright, sunny day and Dutch took a full roll

Fur Seal and Sea Lion

of film, which turned out perfectly. Several times the seal came within five or six feet of him as he hung out of his trolling cockpit and continued to expose film.

That night, our boats tied together in the harbor, we talked again of the friendly little creature. Neither of us could get over the fact that although practically all wildlife is instinctively afraid of man—and considering their brutal treatment at our hands, they certainly have good reason for this—the fur seal had shown no fear of us. It had seemed to want to please, even to communicate with us in some manner—as indeed it had.

The following day we ran into an animal I can kill without the least semblance of guilt—the northern sea lion. I do not mean those graceful, intelligent creatures which put on such talented performances in circuses and marine shows, and which are actually California sea lions instead of seals. I am referring to our northern sea lions, which are ponderous, obese creatures, the bull sometimes reaching nearly a ton in weight. They are belligerent, vicious and extremely intelligent. And they can drive a fisherman berserk. They will follow a troller, staying just out of rifle range (which is not far on a rolling fishing boat), and as soon as he gets a fish on the line, they dash in and snatch it off the hook.

The sea lion does not have the teeth for biting, so he must come to the surface and shake the fish apart, then dive to catch and swallow the slowly sinking pieces. He is then back once more, riding herd, waiting for another fish to steal. It is maddening. A large, persistent sea lion, or perhaps several, can stay with a fisherman all day—and keep his gear clean.

— *THIS RAW LAND* —

Halibut long liners are plagued by them, and a "sea lion bomb," or depth charge, is sometimes used, ostensibly to scare them off. But the sea lions are now wise to them and pay little attention to the small underwater explosions.

Shoot at a sea lion a few times and he will just stick his nose out of the water enough to take a breath when it is necessary for him to come up for air.

To learn how *really* intelligent he is, step on deck with a rifle just as a sea lion surfaces close to the boat, and he will promptly dive. But pick up a broom handle, for instance, and aim it at him as you would a rifle, and he will just glare at you, offering a beautiful shot, as if to say: *Don't you realize, you dumb so-and-so, that I know you can't shoot me with that broom handle!* A persistent sea lion can make you want to slit your wrists, or sit on the hatch with your head in your hands and cry bitterly.

That day off Breakfast Rock a particularly persistent sea lion got on our trail. There was a little southeasterly swell rolling in and it was impossible to hold a bead on the thief; nevertheless, I shot several times in a vain attempt to scare him away. He kept pace with us, lingering behind until we had a fish on, then moved swiftly in beneath the water to take it. For a couple of hours the sea lion terrorized us, until I saw the *Salty* up ahead coming our way. I swung over close and called: "You want a sea lion, ol' buddy?"

Sure enough, Dutch had fish on his lines, and the sea lion began following him. But Dutch, wise to my maneuver, didn't waste any time: he looked up ahead of him, spotted Clell Bacon on the *Romance* coming up the shore from Breakfast Rock, promptly swung over and

Fur Seal and Sea Lion

left the ravenous villain with him, calling: "Hey, Clell, you want a sea lion?"

For a long time afterward we could hear Clell's violent cursing, then every once in a while a frantic fusillade of rifle shots.

I looked at Barb with a wide grin.

"You men are worse than kids, sometimes," she said, and no doubt she was correct in this assumption.

The fishing had dropped off to practically nothing, and it was a lucky fisherman who ended the day with four or five king salmon. We all hung tough, however, for the coho (silver salmon) season had just opened on the Fourth of July and they would begin showing in large schools soon.

Early one morning Lady Luck smiled on me, and off Breakfast Rock five kings hit my lines at the same time. As I fought them one by one and threw them aboard, I was aware of the envious glances of nearby fishermen.

Dutch called over and asked what I'd caught them on. I yelled back and told him, and presently saw him changing lures. On the other side Clell Bacon was doing likewise.

I waited for more kings to hit, but nothing happened. At the end of my pass along the shore I swung around with the others to start back, and out of boredom said to Barb, "Let's have some fun with Dutch."

So, on the off side of the boat, where the others couldn't see me, I hooked the five king salmon back on a line (after making sure there were no sea lions around) and sunk them back into the sea. Then I rigged a cord to one of the tag lines and led it through the pilothouse window where Barb could jerk the pole violently, thus ringing the small cowbell which many of us tied to the tips of our poles.

Now, with the salmon back in the water and Barb at her station, we began our return pass. When we reached the spot where we had caught the salmon, I gave Barb the signal and she began jerking the line furiously, the pole bouncing wildly, the bell ringing steadily.

I glanced at Dutch and Clell on either side of me; they were both watching the bouncing pole.

I appeared nonchalant, first drinking a cup of coffee, then lighting a cigar and smoking leisurely. After a reasonable length of time had elapsed, I began to bring the line in. When I came to the leader with the first dead king dragging behind, I began my masterful pantomime.

After fighting the dead salmon for fully five minutes, I at last worked it close to the boat, then made wild swings at it with my gaff which splashed the water and made it appear—at their distance—as if the king was really fighting. Finally I sunk the gaff hook into its head and dragged it aboard. Then I threw in the gurdy clutch and pulled the line up to the next leader and went through the same procedure.

Clell and Dutch, after dragging precisely the same type lures right alongside of me for several hours without a single fish on deck, were getting tired of lucky Wayne just hauling the fish in from right under their noses.

"What in the hell are you using?" Clell demanded loudly, after I had thrown the last one aboard.

Fur Seal and Sea Lion

I told him, then added innocently: "How are you doing, Clell?"

"I haven't had a goldurn strike yet!" he shouted back, getting more furious all the time.

Dutch had sunk into a silent rage on the other side, working his gear completely over, taking everything off and in desperation trying different kinds of lures.

I knew how they were feeling, for we were not out here purely for sport. In addition to making a living, we are continually fighting the elements, battling the sea lions, sharks, jellyfish, the islands of floating kelp—and just plain bad luck. Then right next to you, a stupid so-and-so, who could not possibly pour sea water out of his boots without spilling it, stumbles blindly into a school of king salmon and picks up $200 in two passes, and you haven't had a strike yet!

Clell and Dutch, desperate now, wheeled in behind me and made passes at the precise spot where I had "hooked" the salmon. I continued on, and began to rehook the kings back on the lines and sink them down again.

"Wayne," Barb said, beginning to feel sorry for Dutch and Clell, "that's enough!"

"Just once more," I said between chuckles.

"It'd serve you right if a sea lion came along and grabbed your fish."

"You know it might happen, too," I said. "Just once more, Barb."

And once more was too much for them. Dutch turned off and began trolling toward the harbor entrance. Clell, however, had had it! He viciously threw in his gurdy clutch and began to put his gear aboard. A few minutes later his poles went up, then blue smoke rose from his stack as he headed for the harbor at full speed.

After a while Pap trolled by. He had been prospecting off Wooden Island, and had only one little king to show for the day. He was on his way to the harbor. I told him of the joke I had played on Dutch and Clell. He laughed, then said he'd shake them up some more. When he got in, he told them he had watched me pull ten more big king salmon in a row!

Barb and I did not get another strike all afternoon, and when we finally pulled our gear aboard and went in to sell, Dutch and Clell were waiting on the buying scow to see our big catch.

I threw the five worn kings in the fish buyer's scales and grinned at them.

Dutch and Clell stepped aboard to see where the *rest* of the salmon were. But there were none.

And now it dawned on them.

"You . . . !" Clell said.

Dutch gave me a pained grin. "I'll get even with you for this, so help me, I will!"

6

Coho Fishermen

One evening in mid-July, a large Fish and Game research vessel came into Port Alexander. The skipper said they had just found an immense school of coho salmon about forty miles off Cape Ommaney. The school had been feeding and slowly working its way toward shore.

This was good news indeed. But how long would it take them to get within our reach? And where would they hit? They could be salmon heading for Canadian waters, or Oregon and Washington fish that might suddenly swerve and continue on southward. All we could do was wait and keep a close watch for them. In the meantime all of the fishermen began to make up their coho gear. For cohos you use smaller spoons and hooks, and space the leaders closer together. The coho seldom weighs more than twelve or thirteen pounds, though these early ones would average less—probably six or seven pounds, since they were still growing.

— *THIS RAW LAND* —

The coho salmon ranges widely from the coastal waters of California northward to the Arctic Ocean, and westward to Kamchatka and Japan. Like the other four species of Pacific Ocean salmon, the coho, after returning from its mysterious sea voyage, heads for the precise stream or river in which it originated, spawns and dies. The coho is considered a three-year fish, but as in the other species, this sometimes varies.

The fishermen spread out now; some prospecting the southern Kuiu shore, some heading for Coronation Island, and still others running directly off shore. We all are searching for feed, and it is the birds who will tell us where the feed is.

One day a boat finds fish off Larch Bay, and the rush is on. Because it is a long run from the harbor to where the fish are, we leave long before daylight, easing single file through the narrow entrance channel until we are out in the clear. We run by compass toward Wooden Island, the glow of running lights on all sides of us now. To the east there is an imperceptible lighting of the sky, and presently we make out the dark shoreline; ahead is the silhouette of Wooden Island.

Barb cooks breakfast and I eat standing at the wheel. We pass between Wooden Island and Cape Ommaney, and begin bucking into a long, easy swell from the southwest. We go around the cape, and there are birds working ahead. Many of the boats slow down to trolling speed and begin to lower their poles. We do likewise, and soon I have the gear out. I breathe deeply of the fresh sea air and watch the first rays of the early-morning sun beginning to break across the rugged

Coho Fishermen

mountain mass of the mainland to the east. At this moment I would not trade places with another soul on earth. Up ahead a patch of needlefish boil briefly on the surface, and the sea birds wheel in with the raucous cries as they dive in to gorge. One of the bow poles begins to bounce, then the other one. I feel my pulse quicken. Now both main poles begin to bounce steadily.

"We're in them!" I call to Barb, and she comes on deck in slacks and boots and a heavy wool shirt to protect her against the early-morning chill. I have been breaking her in to handle the gurdies and to land fish; now I'll need her. She climbs down into the cockpit with me and gets ready. She will work the two lines on her side, and I will handle my two. On each line we have twelve lures, or a total of forty-eight, and at the moment there is possibly a salmon on every hook!

We begin to bring them in and throw them into the bins directly ahead of us. I take twelve cohos off my bow line and put it back down; the fish are hitting the lures as I snap on each leader. By the time I have all twelve lures back on, the line is loaded with fish. Nevertheless, I snap on the tag line and put it back onto the tip of the pole to let the fish work off their edge. Now I start in with the main line.

Meanwhile Barb is landing fish, a bit awkwardly at first, but she relaxes a little and picks up speed. In front of us the bins begin to fill up. . . .

After two hours of pulling fish steadily, the pace slows down, with only a stray coho now and then. As Barb handles the gear, I get out the cleaning trough and begin to dress the fish. The needlefish have gone deep now, and the gulls wheel in behind us, waiting until I throw gills and viscera overboard, then fight savagely for them. Before I am finished dressing the fish we have caught, we run into another school—and suddenly the lines are loaded once more.

Around two in the afternoon, Barb goes inside and makes coffee and sandwiches during a lull, then we are back fishing again. The forward bins are full of dressed fish and I cover them with wet burlap sacks to protect them from the sun.

The afternoon passes swifty for us, and at seven in the evening we begin trolling slowly back around the cape, dressing fish on the way. When we are at last caught up, we pull the gear aboard, raise the poles and run toward the harbor. We wait our turn to sell our catch, then pull alongside the big tender and tie up.

I pitch our catch aboard and the salmon are weighed and dumped into the hold to be iced down in huge bins. The fish buyer totals up our poundage and pays Barb in cash, while I scrub the deck. We move over to the float and tie to Pap and Dutch.

"Well, how did you do?" they ask, and I look questioningly at Barb.

She is tired and there is fish blood splattered over her face, but she grins and says we have made almost $500.

It is a good feeling. I know we will have other good days; I also know we'll have bad days, and that we'll lose time to the fog and storms. But now it is good to relax and drink a highball as we talk of the day.

Barb washes up at the tiny sink and begins supper, although it is now after eleven o'clock.

Dusk comes slowly in this land of long summer

Coho Fishermen

days. We eat, then go to bed, for the alarm will go off in another three hours and we'll be heading out into the darkness for another day of fishing. . . .

The days seemed to fly by, and suddenly August was gone and September was upon us. The cohos had moved across the strait to Port Malmesbury and off Tebenkof Bay, and we moved with them.

On the tenth of September, the cohos were gone —headed up the inside passages to spawn in the creeks and rivers from which they had originated. The season was over.

The boats began to disperse. Some, like Steve Ervin on the *Sea Hog* and Joe Cash on the *Flicka,* pointed their bows south for a week's run back to Seattle. Others returned to their home ports of Ketchikan, Wrangell, Petersburg and Sitka. Barb and I, together with Dutch and Pap, returned to Warm Springs Bay to spend the winter, until the spring snows would melt and the sun would warm our backs as we painted our boats and made the fishing gear ready for another season.

PART TWO

7

Deer and Brown Bear

In the spring two of Barb's friends had come north to visit us, and stayed through the summer helping Ma in Warm Springs Bay. Both were single, attractive young nurses, and it was not long before my brothers began making long runs home to see them. Duke, skipper of a cannery tender out of Excursion Inlet, somehow managed to stop in to see Shirley Illige, a small, dark-haired girl who originally came from Oregon. By summer's end their romance had progressed to the point of marriage, and when Duke was through for the season he and Shirley flew south to be married in her mother's home at Milwaukie, Oregon. In October, Dutch and Joyce LeDuc, a lively outdoor girl from Michigan, were making similar plans.

All of us could not have been more pleased. Pap, Ma and I felt that both girls would fit into our way of life just as Barb had.

While we waited for them to return from their

honeymoons, I took my boat over to Surprise Harbor, and began to hunt the fat Sitka black-tail bucks for winter meat. Barb expected a baby in the spring, and since she had been on the boat all summer, I thought it best that she stay home and rest up a bit. For the first time in many years I was going off on our annual deer hunt alone, but in a way I relished it. It is important for a man to stand alone every so often and look at the country about him, to listen to the wind sigh through the forest or watch the sun come up as he thinks his private thoughts.

Each season of the year has its special appeal, but for me, the early part of October has always been the best. The mornings are clear and crisp, and the no-see-ums and deer flies have vanished. The mountains and the trees of the higher ridges show the first light snows, and winter is not too far ahead. All day long the sky is filled with ducks and geese on the way south from the interior and the far reaches of the Arctic. Many stop to feed and rest in the tidal flats of the bays, and their haunting cries are audible long after dark. Whenever I hear them I am reminded of when, as a voracious reader of eleven or twelve, I had been introduced to *Wild Geese Calling* and heard their cries and first felt the lure of Alaska. It was then I had first dreamed of the land which London, Beach and White wrote about so compellingly.

I arose early each morning, dressed and made coffee, then sat out on the back deck with my coffee cup in hand as I listened to the early-morning sounds about me. I watched the delicate shades of sunrise color the frosty slopes and listened to the mallards and honkers talking it up on the tide flats of the bay.

Deer and Brown Bear

When the sun finally showed its full form above the mainland to the east, I would rise and fry bacon and eggs, top it off with several more cups of coffee and light a cigar. Presently I'd take my .30–06 from over my bunk, check it over, then climb into the skiff alongside and row ashore.

Each day I hunted the old familiar ridges and valleys beyond the harbor. Sometimes in the morning I passed by a good buck simply because I wanted to go on hunting. If I saw one in early afternoon I took him, for it still gave me time to dress and pack him out before darkness caught me in the woods. If I got back to the boat fairly early, I hung the buck from the boom, fixed a quick sandwich, then tried to get up to the grass flats with the shotgun before dark. Those were wonderful days, and they slid by much too quickly. Soon I had several fat bucks hanging on deck, as well as strings of Canadian honkers and teal and mallards.

After my evening fowl hunt, I sat on deck with a highball and tuned my ears to the night sounds as I marveled over the life I lived. At such moments I would not trade places with another soul on earth. This country would not always be so isolated or bountiful, I knew, but while it was I would enjoy it to my fullest capacity.

One evening in Surprise Harbor I had a close call with a brownie. I had anchored the boat in the lee of Deer Island, and because it was too late in the day to go back on the high ridges where the big bucks would be, I rowed ashore on the nearby peninsula and began walking along the shore. I thought I might jump a spike or forked horn for camp meat. I had my .30–06 over one shoulder on the sling, and carried a twelve-gauge pump shotgun in my hand, for if I didn't see any deer, I planned to hit the potholes in the tide flats at dusk and shoot a few ducks or geese.

Presently I came to an alder thicket and began working my way through. Then, as I stepped around a little rocky point I suddenly smelled the strong musky scent of a bear. But it was too late, for I suddenly found myself in an extremely dangerous position: no more than forty feet ahead of me stood an immense she-brownie; twenty feet to my right, a year-and-a-half-old cub curiously studied me. I instantly knew my life probably hung on the actions of this youngster. If the cub decided to run down across the beach directly ahead of me, I could count on the big sow charging.

She gave a sudden *wooof* of warning to the cub, ordering him to clear out fast, then turned a little to one side; I got a glimpse of another large cub in the brush to her left. She swung back now, watching me malevolently, the hair on her back straight up.

At forty feet a man doesn't want to shoot at all, for an enraged bear will be onto him almost before his weapon comes to his shoulder. Here I was with the twelve-gauge shotgun in my hands—a most formidable weapon at close range—but I did not have a cartridge in the chamber. I desperately wanted to jack one in, but I did not dare make the motion or the noise. I stood deathly quiet, waiting for the cub on my right to make his move, hoping it would be the right one and would not infuriate the sow more. The only thing I could hope for if she charged was to pump a shell into the ancient shotgun without it jamming as it sometimes did, and be able to put the charge of number-four shot into the

Deer and Brown Bear

big head before she was onto me. If all went well, I might knock her down and get in another shot or two to finish her off.

A chill suddenly ran down my spine. I waited. The sow woofed again and the cub on my right suddenly wheeled and galloped off into the brush. The other cub obeyed too, and presently they were gone, but it was not over yet. The sow still stood on all fours, hackles raised, just daring me to make a move. I stood like a statue, scarcely breathing.

After what seemed like hours, she turned ponderously, and slowly ambled back into the brush, completely unafraid of the puny creature standing on the beach.

I waited several minutes, then walked a hundred yards down the shoreline until I came to an open stretch. I put down the shotgun and lifted the sling of the .30–06 over my head, jacked a shell into the chamber, and flipped on the safety—just in case. I lit a cigar with shaking fingers and sat down on a smooth rock, trying to calm my pounding heart. I thought of all the close calls I'd had in the past with brownies, wondering how long a man could go living among these creatures before he made the wrong move, or a little bad luck came his way—and *wham*, he'd have had it.

When the cigar was half gone and I was breathing normally again, I lifted the old Model 97 Winchester shotgun and held it in my hands in the same position as when I'd faced the bear. Down the beach about fifteen yards was a big smooth rock. The rock would be the she-bear. Suddenly I began to swing the shotgun to my shoulder, and at the same time pumped the reloading lever back. As I slid the lever into the forward locking position, it stopped halfway. I lowered the shotgun and looked into the half-open loading slot; the worn mechanism had tilted the shell a little too high and it had jammed tightly against the top of the entrance to the chamber.

I extracted the jammed shell and fed it back into the magazine. Taking the defective shotgun by the barrel, I whirled it around like a hammer thrower and flung it as far as I could into the sea. I walked on down the beach with the .30–06 tucked under an arm, wondering about this capricious thing we know as *luck*, thinking about my friend Rod Darnell's ordeal on Chichagof Island. The situation had been similar, but the outcome was a good deal different. . . .

Rod Darnell, a tall, well-built Juneau businessman, was a born outdoorsman. He owned a small cruiser named the *Liability*, and there was not much of southeastern Alaska—particularly the mainland shore south of Juneau, as well as the islands of Admiralty, Kupreanof, Kuiu, Baranof and Chichagof—that he did not know intimately. Rod hunted mountain goats on the mainland; he had a little scow house up a creek in the tide flats of Big John Bay on Kupreanof Island, where he enjoyed fabulous duck and geese hunting, and he had favorite deer-hunting spots on Admiralty Island, as well as many remote trout streams that he fished.

In Whitestone Harbor on Chichagof Island, Rod had a favorite meadow at timberline where the Sitka black-tail bucks fattened in the fall. He had blazed a trail to this little-known meadow and now, with two friends, was headed for the spot. On their backs were

Deer and Brown Bear

camping pack boards and several clean flour sacks; they did not plan to stay overnight, but to shoot their bucks, dress and quarter them, wrap the meat in the flour sacks, and bring it out on the pack boards.

Two hundred yards from the shore Rod met disaster in the form of three brownies. Like the ones I encountered, they were a big she-bear and two cubs a year and a half old. (A she-bear does not give birth every year, but every three years. Cubs born in the spring will not be cast off on their own until their mother mates two years later. Even then the cubs will sometimes linger near her, although she is now pregnant with another litter of one to four cubs, until she deliberately runs them off prior to hibernation.) So, these *cubs*, if we can call a two-hundred-pound bear such, were old enough and mean enough to be formidable enemies themselves.

The two cubs snorted and crashed away into the brush out of Rod's sight as the she-bear huffed her orders. Like most experienced hunters in a party, Rod was not carrying a cartridge in the chamber of his .30–06. He quickly slipped the rifle sling off his shoulder and jacked a cartridge into the chamber; then he called a warning to his hunting companions, Vern Clemons and Ree Reindeau, who, although not far behind him on the brushy trail, did not know of the danger Rod faced not twenty paces ahead. One of them thought he'd jumped a buck.

Rod, old hunter that he was, stood fast, not wanting to shoot unless he absolutely had to; he was hoping that with the cubs safe in the brush, the sow would turn away.

But the hope was in vain. She flattened her ears and came straight for him, great mouth open, roaring wildly in her rage. Few men can realize how fast these awkward-looking beasts can move. Rod had time to fire one shot in the split second before she was on him.

As soon as he pulled the trigger, Rod twisted to the right, dived headfirst into the spongy muskeg, and clasped both arms around the vulnerable area where his skull and spine joined.

The vicious animal was onto him in a second. She bit into his arm, almost tearing it from the socket, and flung it back with a shake of her mighty head. Biting into Rod's shoulder, she lifted him completely clear of the ground, shook him like a rag doll, and flung him back down. The attack was so sudden that despite the damage she had already done to him, he felt no pain at this point. As he hit the ground Rod twisted onto his belly again, instinctively protecting his stomach. One rake of her claws could disembowel him. Once a bloody hand flopped down before his eyes; it looked like a part of a surrealistic painting he'd once seen, and after a moment he realized the gory hand was his.

Like most of us who live in brownie country, Rod knew his only chance was to force himself to lie quietly with his hands clasped over his head, despite the pain that was beginning to course through him. So he "played possum" while the enraged beast tried to tear him to pieces.

Suddenly her teeth clamped down on the back of his skull and she lifted him, shaking him viciously. Bright lights flashed before his eyes and he was in excruciating agony. It felt like his head was being torn

Deer and Brown Bear

from his body. *This is it!* he thought. *I can't take any more!*

But the she-devil wasn't through yet; she continued shaking him, flailing his body against the ground. A pair of binoculars which hung around his neck on a strap were pounding his chest as she shook him, beating the breath from him.

Suddenly there was an explosion, and he was flung away. After he worked up the courage to raise his bloody head and look around, he saw the bear was down. Vern Clemons had shot the beast off of him, and now he watched as Ree Reindeau put his rifle muzzle against the bear's massive head and pulled the trigger. It was all over.

Vern and Ree dropped on their knees, and Rod saw the horror in their eyes as they looked at him. They lit a smoke for him, and put it gently in his mouth, hands trembling as they tore up the flour sacks and tried to stem the blood that spurted from his many wounds.

Now the battle to save his life was just beginning. They had to get him back to the *Liability*, but they had no radiophone and Rod would bleed to death if they didn't get a doctor to him very soon. They bandaged his chest and shoulders and badly lacerated neck. Part of his scalp hung down over one ear, and they folded it back in place and wrapped strips of the flour sacks around his head to hold it in position.

They finally got him to the beach, then rowed out to the *Liability*. It was a seventy-mile run to town—out of the question. Rod told them to pull the anchor and run toward the cannery at Funter Bay.

Luck was with them now; out in Chatham Strait

they saw the mailboat, *Forrester,* on its weekly run to Tenakee Hot Springs, and they hailed Captain Don Gallagher and told him of the disaster. Gallagher promptly called Juneau on his radiophone and within a few minutes had a plane and doctor on their way. . . .

Not long ago I was talking to Rod about his ordeal and asked him why it had taken so long for his hunting companions to shoot the she-bear off him.

"Well," he said, "it *did* seem to me like hours before Vern shot, but when I later asked them how long they judged it to be between the time the bear first grabbed me and when Vern finally killed it—you know what they both said?"

"What?"

"Thirty seconds."

By the time Duke and Dutch brought their brides home in late October, I had made several trips to Surprise Harbor, and the freezer was now full of meat. Ma and Barb were canning venison, and Pap, the smoked-ham and sausage specialist, was busy in the smokehouse.

My brothers, after the confines of the cities, were anxious to sight in their rifles and make a trip to Surprise Harbor. The trapping season would open on the first of December, and this trip was to check over our trapping grounds that ran from Bartlett Point on the east tangent of Surprise Harbor, around the harbor shoreline to Point Gardner and then to Wilson Cove, where we met the Thlinget Indian trappers from Angoon.

A few days later we were back and getting our

Deer and Brown Bear

trapping gear together. Our ground had shown an unusual amount of mink and otter sign, and with the rumor of good prices this season, we hoped to do very well. One day a week before the season opened we were ready to go.

8

The Trappers

Because Surprise Harbor was mostly open to the southeasterly storms that rolled up Chatham Strait from the open sea, we decided not to take one of the big boats. Instead, we would load all of our equipment on the *Vanguard,* and Pap would take us and our gear over to Surprise Harbor and leave us there.

On a crisp morning in the latter part of November, we said good-by to our wives and sailed out of Warm Springs Bay, the afterdeck of the *Vanguard* piled high with equipment and provisions. Here is a list of what we had:

>wood-burning cookstove
>stovepipe
>two-burner propane hot plate with tank
>chain saw
>axes, splitting mall, wedges
>sleeping bags and air mattresses
>cooking utensils, dishes, etc.

The Trappers

    herring gill net
    50 pounds of rock salt
    large supply of paper plates
    half case of paper towels
    50 mink pelt stretcher boards with wedges
    15 otter pelt stretcher boards with wedges
    3 mink fleshing poles
    2 otter fleshing poles
    350 mink traps
    50 toothed otter traps
    enough food staples for a month, including bacon, eggs, canned vegetables, etc.
    4 quarts of 150-proof rum
    rifles and ammunition
    skinning and fleshing knives
    good supply of extra wool clothing
    10-horsepower Mercury outboard motor
    spare propeller and spark plugs, tools
    two 50-gallon drums of mixed gasoline
    hand-barrel pump

    When we arrived in Surprise Harbor, Pap eased the *Vanguard* up the head of the bay until we could see bottom. We dropped the anchor, unloaded the mountainous pile of groceries and equipment into the skiff and ran it ashore. This took several trips with the skiff, and when at last this was completed, Pap looked at the low arcing sun just sliding out of sight behind Baranof Island to the west, and said: "I'd better be heading for home, boys. When do you want me back?"

    I looked at my brothers. "How about a week after the season opens?" I asked. "That will give us time to have a real nice shipment of furs to go. What do you boys say?"

"Sounds good to me," Duke answered. "If the weather is good you can cross the strait a day or two before the mailplane is due at home, and we can get the first batch of furs stateside quick and maybe get a good price."

"All right," Pap said, and began to pull the anchor. A moment later he was steaming out of Surprise Harbor into Chatham Strait.

We ran the skiff back to the beach and Duke and I began to carry our gear to the little scow house where we would live. In *The Cheechakoes,* I described this amphibious dwelling that had once been a flourishing bordello.

While Duke and I carried the bedding and clothing and groceries inside, Dutch ran the skiff over to a deepwater point about two hundred yards from camp and rigged an anchor and buoy with a small pulley on it, so we could pull the skiff out into deep water to leave it.

We had timed our arrival at high tide, so that we would not have to carry our gear far. Dutch came back to check the two fifty-gallon drums of mixed gasoline we had dumped over the *Vanguard*'s side into the sea. We had floated them to the beach and tied them up, and now Dutch pulled them up as far as they would come and tied the lines to a tree. As soon as the tide went out and left them high and dry, we would roll them up above the high-water mark and tip them up.

Even on the 57th parallel the winter days are short; it doesn't begin to get light until nine-thirty in the morning, and by three-thirty it begins to get dark again. It was almost dark now, as Duke and I wrestled the cast-iron wood cookstove into the float house and set it up.

The Trappers

While Duke climbed up on the roof to put on a couple of lengths of stovepipe, I lit a gas lantern and hooked up the inside stovepipe. Meanwhile the Dutchman had taken the chain saw and cut several blocks of wood from a big drift log on the beach, and was splitting it. I went down to get an armload, and as I started back, big lazy flakes of snow began to drift down from the dark sky.

With a fire burning briskly in the stove, and a teakettle full of water heating, we took the lantern out and began to carry the rest of our equipment into the protective lean-to on one end of the shack.

It was pitch-dark by the time we finished, and we went inside and began to get everything shipshape. As Duke and I put the groceries and personal gear away, the Dutchman began to prepare supper. I could never figure out just where he had picked up his knack for cooking, but he had it, and Duke and I would pack water and wash dishes or do anything else just to have him do the cooking.

Tonight he put a little cooking oil into the bottom half of the Dutch oven, then threw in some rice and browned it just so. Next came tomato paste, water, onions, dried pimento and bell peppers, various spices, two cans of mushrooms, a touch of this and that, and finally three cans of Dungeness crabmeat. Soon the wonderful aroma of the jambalaya filled the shack.

Duke, who was the hot-buttered-rum specialist, broke open a bottle and began to mix the drinks. A moment later we were all sitting back on our crude wooden benches, sipping the hot drinks as we waited for the jambalaya to finish.

"Boys," I said, "I think we're going to have one hell of a good season this year, judging from the sign."

Duke nodded. "Main thing now is—will we get a fair price?"

This was the big thing. When we had first come to Alaska in 1946, otter pelts had sold for forty and fifty dollars, mink up to forty, and martens as high as sixty dollars! In recent years prices had dropped to less than half on otter and mink, and we turned marten out of our traps because the fur buyers didn't want them—they were not fashionable any more.

As we sipped our hot rum, we studied the various brochures the fur buyers had sent out, as we had done again and again during the past few days, trying to make up our minds about who to ship our furs to. This year there was one fur buyer whose name stood uniquely alone: *O'Callahan!*

"I'm kinda for trying O'Callahan," Dutch said at last.

"We might as well," Duke said, frowning in concentration, "but you know, I'll bet that O'Callahan is Bernstaus' or Goldberg's brother starting up a fur-buying company on his own. What do you think, Wayne?"

"It's certainly possible."

The next morning after breakfast, Duke and Dutch slung their rifles over their shoulders and took off down the beach. They wanted to scout for mink sign around Sign Bay. We hadn't brought any fresh meat with us, so each planned to shoot a fat doe and bring it back for camp meat. The bucks were now in rut, and strong.

After they had gone, I got things ready to "tan" our traps. We had brought an empty fifty-gallon drum with the top cut out for this job. I dug a shallow hole not far

The Trappers

from our shack, rimmed it with big rocks from the beach, and built a fire. Now I placed the empty drum over the fire, and filled it with fresh water from the creek. While the water heated, I took an axe and went back into the woods to strip bark from hemlock trees. When I had accumulated a pile of bark, I carried it back and dumped it into the barrel of water.

By the time the boys returned that afternoon with does on their backs, I finally had the water boiling, and after hanging the deer up in our lean-to, we began "tanning" our traps, a bunch at a time.

This tanning, as we call it, does two things: it replaces whatever odor the traps have with the hemlock or "woods" smell. The acid in the hemlock also gives the steel a protective coating that helps keep them from rusting too badly—much like the bluing of a rifle barrel. When we had finished we hung the traps beneath a big spruce tree behind the shack until we would need them.

Although we used trail sets a great deal, we also made bait sets in some spots. One afternoon Dutch saw a small patch of herring flipping off the point where we kept the skiff anchored. We broke out the herring gill net and set it. The next morning it was full of herring, which we salted to preserve because the temperature was above freezing.

The night before the season opened we brought the ten-horsepower Mercury outboard motor into the shack and went over it. We checked the ignition points, put in new spark plugs, and took the carburetor apart and cleaned it meticulously. Now we were ready. We went to bed that night full of excitement, hardly able to wait for morning.

— THIS RAW LAND —

We were up long before daylight, ate by lantern light, and got everything ready to go. At first light we carried our traps out and loaded them into the skiff. With Duke in the stern running the outboard, we headed out the bay. The sea was calm, with only a slight northeasterly swell.

Our plan was this: They would drop me off at Bartlett Point, and I would set traps back toward camp. Duke would take advantage of the calm sea and run around Point Gardner to our line shack, which was located about halfway between the point and Wilson Cove. He would drop Dutch off with one hundred mink traps and a sleeping bag; Dutch would set fifty traps from the line camp toward Wilson Cove, then tomorrow he would start with the other fifty traps and set back toward Point Gardner. He carried with him several sandwiches wrapped in wax paper, as well as some candy bars to hold him over until tomorrow night.

Duke would then come back into Surprise Harbor, anchor the skiff off Sign Bay, and set traps back toward our camp.

It is exciting to ferret out the mink trails and runways and try to figure out the best places to set your traps. Mink and otter make their living from the sea, feeding on small fishes and crabs. One of the mink's favorite foods is the sea urchin, a round, spiny little creature the size of a biscuit. The sea urchin lives on the shallow, rocky bottom of the sea, and coastal mink make use of the extremely low tides to harvest them and carry them back to their dens and feeding spots to eat.

When a man is setting traps in country he has previously trapped, he remembers many old sets that

The Trappers

were used before; all of this ground was well known to me, and I made good time. There was an abundance of sign; well-used trails, as well as freshly eaten sea-urchin shells scattered here and there, and I was confident I'd do well.

By the time I finally worked my way to our camp, it was completely dark, and I was stumbling over the rocky beach. I went inside and lit a gas lantern, put water on the propane hot plate to heat, then built a fire in the wood stove. As I began to slice venison steaks for supper, I heard the sound of the outboard motor out in the darkness of the bay. I took a hand lantern and walked down the beach to meet Duke.

"By golly, she sure looks good over my way," he said, as we pulled the skiff out on its anchor line. "Sign all over the place!"

"Same thing on my ground," I replied. "You get your fifty traps all set?"

"Yeah, just barely . . . was getting dark on me, though."

"I wonder how ol' Dutchman made out today?" I said idly while we walked toward the lights of the shack.

Duke shook his head. "I just hope this weather holds up—and don't freeze all our traps up."

At daybreak the next morning we were off in the skiff again with another fifty traps each. I was going to drop Duke and his traps off on the far side of his line at Sign Bay, and he would set toward Point Gardner. I would anchor the skiff off the sandy beach this side of Gardner and set around the point itself and on down the shore until I met Dutch.

When Duke finished setting his traps, he should

end up fairly close to where I'd left the skiff. He would run around the point with the skiff until he met Dutch and me walking back along the beach, and pick us up.

After we put away enough venison steaks to keep a logging crew going that night, Dutch sat back and sighed, then rolled a cigarette. "Boys," he said, "there's sign all over that shore down there. There's enough sets left for another seventy-five traps."

"Well, we don't have them," Duke said. "Besides, I've seen sign like this before—and you get hardly anything. They move, or something."

"We'll know tomorrow," I said.

The wind woke us early the next morning, slashing furiously against our little shack, rattling windows and blowing empty gas cans around in the lean-to. I got up and stoked the fire. The wind continued to increase, until gusts of seventy and eighty miles per hour were shaking the shack.

Duke, sitting up in his sleeping bag, was smoking a cigarette. "Boy, am I glad we didn't bring one of the big boats!" he said. "We'd be dragging anchor all over the bay."

"Won't be any chance to use the skiff today," I said, making coffee on the propane hot plate. "We'll have to run what traps we can in the bay."

Duke nodded. "Me and Dutchman will check traps from here on to Gardner—and we better get to humpin' if we're going to make it back before dark tonight!"

I dressed and fixed breakfast: thin-sliced venison steaks, four eggs each, biscuits and flour gravy, all topped off with a big pot of coffee.

As soon as we finished we put on our wool caps and

The Trappers

gloves and coats, and with a burlap sack beneath our pistol belts, we headed out into the darkness, flashlights in our hands to show us the way until daylight came.

When I could make out the shape of the shoreline, I left the flashlight on a prominent rock, to be picked up on my return, and trotted along the beach. From time to time my eye would go to spots where I had traps set, and I would sometimes see a movement of fur. I kept on, however, walking awhile, then trotting again until I came at last to the end of my line.

I had six traps set along trails leading toward the sea; there had been a good show of sea-urchin shells when I'd set, and now as I came to the first set, I saw the ground was torn up where the trap had been. The ring in the end of the chain was tied with nylon cord to the base of a small tree, and led out of sight beneath a log. I pulled my .22 pistol from the holster with one hand, and reached down and began pulling the chain slowly from beneath the log; out came the mink, a big male with a foreleg caught in the trap. I feinted several times at the hissing mink, then rapped him sharply across the top of the head with my pistol barrel. Putting a boot directly across his rib cage, I pressed down. I returned my pistol to the holster, released the dead mink's foot from the trap, and reset it in the same spot, carefully raking the torn-up trail back into place and covering the set trap lightly with spruce needles and moss. Now on to the next one.

Out of those six traps I had four mink. I put them into the burlap sack, threw it over my shoulder, and went on down the line. This was where the excitement came, going from one trap to another, wondering what there would be at the next, the time flying swiftly by, unnoticed, until the low arcing sun to the west reminded me it would be dark soon.

Finally I came to a steep hill behind the beach where I had set otter traps around their slides and dens; out of ten traps I had three otters. I approached the first one cautiously with a heavy branch in my hands for a club. An otter is extremely playful by nature, but trapped and cornered it is at once transformed into a vicious and deadly creature that would tear you apart in an instant if given the chance. A number of years ago a trapper on the west coast of Prince of Wales Island crawled under some overhanging brush and prepared to set a trap in front of what appeared to be an otter den. There before him lay two weathered skeletons; one was a man's, and at his throat lay the bones of an otter, one leg bone still held in the jaws of a rusted trap.

Wet with sweat from fighting the three otters, I reset the last trap and began to move on, for it was now getting dark. I tied the otters' feet together and slung them over my shoulder like furry bed rolls; over the other shoulder I carried the burlap sack with fourteen mink in it.

I walked back along the beach to where I had left the flashlight this morning, picked it up, and went around the point. Ahead, across the flats was the dim outline of our shack. I stumbled along under the weight of the mink and otter, glad that it wasn't much farther.

Far across on the opposite shore I saw the bobbing of another light. I wondered if it had gone as well for my brothers today....

9

Christmas

I was building a fire in the wood stove when Duke staggered into the lean-to and dumped his heavy sack on the floor. A moment later he sat down on one of the benches with a sigh of relief.

"Where's the Dutchman?" I asked.

Duke took out a smoke and lit it. "We picked up twenty-two mink and six otters," he said, "and ol' Dutch got so excited thinking about his traps on the other side of Point Gardner, he decided to cross the pass and run his line tomorrow."

It sounded like Dutch; he was a real "mountain man." Here was what he had proposed to do: with only three hours of daylight left, he had headed back into the woods and began to climb the steep hills that separate Surprise Harbor from Chatham Strait. He would cross the fairly heavy snows of the pass and go down the other side. Somewhere along the way he'd shoot the head off a ptarmigan, and when darkness stopped him, he would build a fire, roast and eat the bird, then shiver and stomp around the fire in the freezing night until it became light enough to travel. He'd run the far end of his trapline and get into our line shack that night. If he'd had the good fortune to kill another ptarmigan, he'd eat that. If not, he would dig clams at low tide and cook them in the coals of another fire, then skin out what mink he had, roll up the pelts and put them into the burlap sack he carried. The next morning he would be off at daybreak and run the rest of his traps. If the weather was such that we could use the skiff and outboard motor, he would be looking for us to pick him up somewhere on the other side of the Point Gardner shore. If the sea was too rough for the skiff, he would simply cross the pass again and hike back to camp, perhaps spending another night in the woods!

"You sure didn't carry twenty-two mink and six otter back with you!" I said to Duke.

"Not hardly," Duke said, fixing our nightly hot-buttered rums. "I cached the otter at Sign Bay. I hope we'll be able to use the skiff tomorrow and pick them up."

When supper was finished we lit another gas lantern, and the work began. Duke, after sharpening his pocket knife, brought in a sack of mink and dumped them out on the floor. We each took a mink in our laps and began to skin it. Once a man becomes used to it, he can skin a mink in a very short time. Duke and I worked until all thirty-six mink had been skinned; then I made a pot of coffee and we relaxed for a few minutes before beginning to flesh the pelts. For this a round fleshing pole, tapered on one end, is used. You turn the pelt inside out and pull it tightly over the fleshing pole and tack the hind feet and tail down. Then you use a dull-bladed knife to scrape all of the fat and oil from the pelt.

Christmas

This was what the half case of paper towels were for: to catch the strips of fat and to wipe the oil from the skins when we were finished fleshing them. Then the pelt goes onto a stretcher board with the flesh side still out, the tail and feet tacked down; it is propped against the wall for the night. In the morning, before the pelt is fully dry, it is turned with the fur side out and slipped back on the board. A thin wooden wedge is slipped tight beneath the belly, so that when the skin has completely dried, the wedge can be pulled, loosening the pelt enough to slip it from the stretching board. We had four sizes of boards: small, medium, large and extra-large. An extra-large male mink will measure thirty-seven to forty inches from head to tip of tail when stretched and dried. And it is not uncommon for a large otter pelt to measure six feet or more from tip to tip, but we did not get the otter pelts fleshed that night. At four A.M. we finished skinning them, and then rolled the pelts and stored them where they would stay cool. After carting the mink and otter carcasses out into the wood, we washed up and rolled, utterly beaten, into our sleeping bags.

Before I dropped off to sleep, I listened to the savage gusts of wind whining in the treetops and thought of the Dutchman out there somewhere hunkered around an open fire, burning on one side and freezing on the other, as he waited impatiently for daylight. . . .

It was still blowing hard from the southeast the next morning, and we could not use the skiff. Duke and I walked along the beach to Sign Bay and checked some of his traps, then picked up the six otters he had cached the day before and carried them in.

That evening we skinned and fleshed our catch and

put the pelts onto stretcher boards. When we finally finished and went to bed the gusts of wind were strong as ever, and we could hear the sound of the surf breaking on the beach in front of the shack. I lay there thinking of Dutch on the other side of the mountains, hoping that the wind would let up enough by morning so we could use the skiff to run around Point Gardner and pick him up.

When the alarm clock went off at seven, the sound of the wind was gone. While Duke built a fire, I stepped outside into the dark and listened for the surf; there was only the gentle sound of wavelets against the sandy beach.

"Sounds like we'll be able to use the skiff today," I told Duke, and started breakfast while he turned the mink pelts fur side out and put them back on the stretcher boards.

At daylight we were off in the skiff. I dropped Duke off to run the rest of his line, and then went on to where I had begun setting traps on the far side of him. I anchored the skiff out for him to pick up, and went down the beach toward Point Gardner.

By three o'clock that afternoon I had finished, and was sitting on a rocky point smoking, when I saw Dutch coming down the beach with his burlap sack over one shoulder. When he came up to me I grinned at him and said, "Well, how'd she go, ol' buddy?"

"Pretty good," Dutch said, and slipped the sack off his shoulder. He sat down and rolled a smoke, then went on: "I got twenty-five mink and four otter—left the otter cached; we can run down with the skiff and pick them up. When's Duke coming?"

Christmas

"Should be along any time now."

We smoked for another few minutes, talking about our lines, and presently heard the sound of the outboard motor. We stood up and waved our caps until Duke spotted us against the dark shore, and turned in to pick us up.

Again we worked most of the night skinning and fleshing and stretching the pelts on the boards. When we made a count we found we had seventy-eight mink and fourteen otter pelts for the three-day period. Not bad!

The first four days of trapping take the "gravy" from a trapline; then it will settle down to a slow but steady production.

By the time Pap came over to pick up our first batch to ship south, we had 164 mink and 30 otter pelts.

As Pap prepared to leave, he asked: "Well, who do you want me to ship them to?"

"I'm still for trying O'Callahan," Dutch said, looking at Duke and me.

"That's fine with me." Duke said.

"All right," I told Pap, "but tell friend O'Callahan to wire us an offer immediately. If we don't like what he's offering we'll send them somewhere else."

"Fine," Pap said. "Now, then, when do you want me back?"

"Two days after the season's over—that'll be the second of January. We'll have all of our traps pulled and be ready to go by then. But if the weather is bad," I told Pap, "just hold off until you get a good day."

Pap nodded and carried our furs inside the cabin of the *Vanguard*. A moment later he was headed home.

Our days fell into routine and slipped away so quickly that when Dutch said, "You boys know, tomorrow is Christmas!" we could hardly believe it.

Immediately we began to prepare for the event. I kept a close lookout for ptarmigan as I ran my trapline, and when I spotted tracks in the slight snow that afternoon, I followed them back into the woods until I came upon a covey of the snow-white birds. They regarded me stupidly as I pulled out my pistol and began to shoot their heads off.

Dutch, the master of outdoor cuisine, was busy Christmas morning baking cherry and apple pies, while Duke and I took care of the rest of the pelts. When the pies were done he made dressing, stuffed the three ptarmigan, and put them into the oven. On top of the stove in a Dutch oven was a boned venison loin rolled up with a layer of dressing, and tied with a string. There were candied sweet potatoes, mashed Irish potatoes, canned asparagus and fruit salad.

Duke mixed up eggnog batter and poured in a bottle of brandy that Pap had brought over.

"Boys," Duke said, lifting his coffee mug of Christmas cheer, "to a hell of a good way of life. I'm glad the majority of the masses don't know what they're missin'!"

"I'll drink to that!" The Dutchman cried. "To many more years of the same!"

Up went the mugs.

"To our luck in finding wives that'll fit into our way of life," I said. "And may we all have sons to follow in our footsteps!"

Up went the mugs. . . .

After stuffing ourselves with Dutch's sumptuous

Christmas

Christmas dinner, I lit a cigar and went out to my tool box in the lean-to. I dug around for a while and came back in with a breast drill and the suction cup from a valve-grinder.

"What's up?" the Duke said, eying me curiously.

"I'm going to make ice cream," I said.

Instantly my brothers saw what I had in mind.

I fitted the shaft of the rubber suction cup into the chuck of the breast drill, while Dutch washed out an empty lard pail and mixed ice cream batter in it. Duke brought in a bucket and a washpan of snow. We set the lard pail into the bucket and packed snow and rock salt around it; then, sticking the suction cup onto the top of the lard pail, I began to crank the breast drill.

Half an hour later we were having cherry pie à la mode.

Then, as dusk began to creep across this lonely land of ours, we began to open presents from our wives and our parents. . . .

10

Sea Voyage

Near the end of December the good weather suddenly deserted us; the southeasterly wind that had kept the temperature slightly above freezing switched to northerly and the thermometer dropped overnight to twenty degrees above zero. The next day it went down to zero, then ten below!

Our sets froze solid and even a heavy otter could practice the Mexican hat dance on top of a trap without setting the trigger pin off. It was infuriating, but we had been lucky to have fine trapping weather for most of the season. On the thirtieth of December we began to chop our traps from the frozen ground and to bring them in. The bitter north wind howled savagely down Chatham Strait, building up great white combers in the unrestricted 150 miles of water that ran all the way to Skagway. There was no chance to use the skiff in such a sea, so we packed all of the traps from Surprise Harbor in on our backs. And then, as the days went by and

Sea Voyage

still there was no letup, we began to carry Dutch's traps across the pass in small bunches at a time—anything to break the bleak monotony of the shack.

When this was accomplished, and still the north wind continued, we sat in our shack and alternately played cards and read. Then came the day when we had devoured every bit of reading material, and sat there thumbing aimlessly through a magazine on the off-chance we might have overlooked something. We were tired of playing cards and tired of looking at each other's faces. In desperation we would stalk out of the shack and patrol the lonely, wind-swept beach, but with no real aim now, just marking time, waiting for the cursed wind to stop so Pap could come and get us.

Few people, unless they have experienced it, can realize how a person's morale can deteriorate with such enforced idleness. When we had been busy trapping, we were completely happy, but now we began to do *anything* to break the dreary monotony. We would whittle for a while, perhaps play pinochle until we tired of that, then tramp the beach aimlessly, as we burned up a little energy and killed time.

For eight solid days it blew without letup. We had by now begun to run low on groceries. Not that we would go hungry, for there was no shortage of deer and ptarmigan, but some of the luxuries such as sugar, eggs, flour, coffee and tea were about gone. Two days later they *were* gone.

Finally, on the fourteenth day after it began to blow from the north, the wind suddenly stopped one night. Duke had gotten up to stoke the fire, and didn't hear the wind in the trees behind the shack. He stepped outside, and it was deathly quiet. He came back in and awoke Dutch and me. We got up and brewed a bunch of used tea bags, then began to get our gear ready to go. We were jubilant; we knew Pap would take advantage of this break in the weather and be over to pick us up today.

Daylight came at last, and we began to move our gear out onto the beach. We let the fire in the stove go out, took it down and carried it out to be loaded aboard the *Vanguard*.

Pap hadn't come by noon, and we became uneasy.

"He'll be here at high tide," I predicted, which was at two o'clock. But two o'clock came and went, then three, and still Pap was not in sight. At three-thirty it was beginning to get dark again.

"Well, he's not coming," I said. "Let's get the stove back into the shack and build a fire; I'm frozen solid." We had been stomping around in the snow of the beach in near-zero weather to keep warm.

"Let's wait a little longer," Duke said.

At four-thirty it was dark, and we could not see any running lights from the *Vanguard*. We carried the stove back inside the shack and set it up again. I started a fire, and began to put together a venison stew.

"I wonder what's wrong?" Duke said, voicing the worry all of us had. Could there have been an accident at home? Was someone seriously ill? Perhaps Pap started out in the *Vanguard* and had engine trouble or something. Could he be drifting out there in the strait somewhere at this very moment?

There was a radiophone at home, and Ma had a nightly schedule with the Alaska Communication Service

Sea Voyage

in Juneau, but if the water wheel or the generator had gone out, they would be unable to contact Juneau. There were still the radiophones on the boats, but sometimes in the winter weather, conditions were so bad you could not make contact with anyone.

As I fixed supper, we would step outside every now and then and peer into the darkness, hoping to see the mast light of the *Vanguard* coming around Point Gardner.

At midnight we went to bed, each of us more worried than we cared to admit. Something was definitely wrong at home, or Pap would have been over—wouldn't he?

"What are we going to do tomorrow, boys?" Dutch asked at last.

"I'm for taking our sleeping bags and furs and trying to make it home in the skiff," Duke said. "That is, if the weather isn't any worse in the morning."

"What do you think, Wayne?" Dutch asked.

I thought it over. "I'm against it. Anyone who tries to cross Chatham Strait in the middle of the winter with a skiff and outboard motor is nuts! And you know it, Duke!"

"What do you propose, then—to sit here on our behinds and wait? What if someone's hurt or seriously sick? Why, Pap may have even had a heart attack!"

All this could be true, I knew. Pap had had a mild stroke the past summer. "I don't know what to say," I finally answered. "Let's look at it again in the morning."

I don't think any of us slept much that night. I lay there trying to decide what we should do, for I knew Duke would be ready to take off into a howling storm by morning. In previous years we could have gone to the cannery in Murder Cove, where a winter watchman had been stationed, and perhaps have made contact with home on their radiophone, but the company had ceased operations this past fall and moved their equipment to Kake, on Kupreanof Island.

When morning came at last, we rose to a dreary world. Fine snow slanted down from the east-northeast, obscuring everything.

"Let's go!" Duke said. "If it's snowin' it won't be blowin'!"

"The hell you say! It can do anything this time of year."

He looked at me, then turned to face Dutch. "I'm for trying it. What do you say, Dutchman?"

"Up to you guys."

"I'm going to try it," Duke said with finality.

"All right," Dutch said, and began packing our furs.

I nodded assent, but I didn't like it. Ahead of us were fifteen miles of water, and we were to cross it in a fourteen-foot skiff loaded down with three men, our bed rolls and furs, plus enough gasoline to make the trip. To start off in clear weather would have been foolhardy, I felt, but to attempt it now in a snowstorm and run by pocket compass would be inviting disaster.

Nevertheless, we wrapped our furs in a waterproof canvas, rolled our sleeping bags, and began to put what remaining food we had into a box. Presently we were ready, and we carried everything down to the beach to the skiff and stowed it away. A few minutes later Duke started the outboard motor, with the pocket compass in his lap, and we headed out into the flying snow.

We set a course for Point Gardner. With the load,

Sea Voyage

we estimated our speed to be four knots, and when forty-five minutes had gone by and we hadn't picked up Point Gardner, we stopped the outboard motor and listened. Faintly we heard the sound of the surf beating off our starboard bow. Duke took a compass bearing and started the outboard motor again.

Ten minutes later we were able to see the dim outline of Point Gardner rock, then the white-painted frame of the light itself. Duke skirted the kelp field and headed out into the white void again, the course due west.

The wind was out of the northeast at perhaps fifteen miles per hour, and the flat-bottomed skiff wallowed abominably in the choppy seas. We had stretched a canvas over the bow and lashed it tightly down to protect our bed rolls and furs. Every now and then we would take spray aboard, and in the near-zero weather, it promptly froze. On we ran, hunched over in our parkas, feet like blocks of ice in our boots.

When Duke got a charley horse from his cramped position, we traded places, and I held the compass on my lap and steered due west. The wind began to pick up now, and presently white caps began to appear about us. Every now and then a comber would catch the skiff wrong and break over the outboard well. Duke and Dutch would bail the water out of the bottom of the skiff without a word. There was no need to speak, for there was nothing to say. Once we had left the protection of Point Gardner, we were irrevocably committed; there was no chance of bucking the wind back into Surprise Harbor.

A capricious thing, this sea; mother of all life, violent and serene by turns, totally unpredictable. . . .

Duke checked his pocket watch, and said something.

"What?" I yelled.

"Should be almost halfway across!" he called back into the wind.

The sea and wind were getting worse by degrees, and I felt the first real twinge of fear. All about us the endless flakes of snow sped ahead of the wind. Water began to break steadily over the stern, splashing the outboard as it came aboard, and ice began to build up. Ahead of me my brothers mechanically bailed the water out of the bottom of the skiff, silent now.

Duke turned and met my glance, and I understood what was in his mind, but it did not matter now. The only thing we could do was to go on and hope our luck held.

"Look!" Dutch shouted, pointing off our starboard beam. "The *Vanguard!*"

And so it was, the dim silhouette of the hull was moving through the snowstorm like a phantom.

"Yo-hooooooo!" Dutch shouted, and I wheeled the ice-laden skiff around into the trough, heading straight for the *Vanguard*.

It disappeared for a moment in the white void, and we strained our eyes to pick up its shape again. When we did it was with the belated realization that the boat was swiftly moving away from us. The boys jumped to their feet and frantically waved their arms and shouted themselves hoarse.

"Shoot!" Duke cried to Dutch, and Dutch reached beneath the canvas on the bow and brought out his rifle. He threw a cartridge into the chamber and shot into the air until the magazine was empty, but the *Vanguard* promptly slipped into the curtain of snow and disappeared.

Sea Voyage

We all sat in utter dejection; it had been *so* close.

The outboard motor began to miss now, running raggedly on one cylinder, and our speed was cut in half. Several inches of water slooshed in the bottom of the skiff, and the boys began to bail furiously as I eased the skiff around on a westerly heading again.

It was soon evident that we must stop and take out the fouled spark plug.

"Where are those spare spark plugs?" I yelled to them.

Dutch took the tool box from under the tarp and began to go through it.

"Find them?"

Dutch shook his head. "Must have forgotten them!"

"Dammit, they were laying there on the table!" I shouted. "Didn't anyone pick them up?"

In our hurry to be off we had forgotten the spark plugs. I stopped the outboard and told Duke to tie a line on the bail of a bucket and throw it over for a sea anchor. The drag of the bucket in the water pulled the bow around into the wind and gave me a chance to work on the engine. With a crescent wrench I broke the ice from the engine cover and unsnapped it. Working with numb hands I unscrewed the spark plugs, one by one, and began to clean the carbon from them with my knife blade.

Each sea that broke on the bow put water into the skiff, and the boys bailed steadily. Suddenly a big one caught us and the sea poured over the bow canvas and into the skiff.

"Hurry!" Duke cried. "One more like that will finish us!"

Holding tightly onto each spark plug, I bent over the

engine and screwed them into the head, one by one. I tightened them with the wrench, snapped on the magneto wires, and put the cover back on. I breathed a prayer it would start and pulled on the starting cord. It barked sharply, and on the next pull it started. Duke pulled the bucket in from the bow, and away we went.

Within fifteen minutes we were again running on one cylinder. The sea was so rough we dared not stop again. The only thing to do was keep on running before the wind and seas. On and on we went at our snail's pace, each of us hunched over a little more in our parkas against the bitter cold, each silent.

Pap would continue on to Surprise Harbor and anchor the *Vanguard;* then he would row ashore and find our note saying we'd left. Immediately he would turn and head back—but would he have a chance of finding us in such weather? I doubted it.

Once that afternoon the snow lifted to the west and we could see Baranof Island perhaps three miles off our portside. We were still chugging along, barely making headway with the ebb tide pushing us down Chatham Strait, and if Pap missed us on his return from Surprise Harbor, our only recourse was to try to make the Baranof shore and spend the night on the beach. We had burned twenty gallons of gasoline, and there was only a five-gallon tin left—not enough to make it home even if the outboard kept running.

Just before dark began to close in, the snow stopped and we could look back and see the light at Point Gardner. It did not appear that we were making any headway against the strong ebb tide. The sound of a foghorn came

Sea Voyage

to us then, barely audible above the noise of the outboard motor.

"Look!" Duke cried, pointing to the southeast. There was the *Vanguard* perhaps a half-mile away. Both Duke and Dutch got out their rifles and began to shoot. The wail of the foghorn seemed to answer, and then we saw the boat turn in our direction.

After a little it stopped and we heard the horn again. I knew then that Pap had heard the shot, but he hadn't spotted us yet. He was shutting the engine off as he blew the horn and listened.

"Keep shooting!" I yelled.

Then the *Vanguard* headed our way again. Presently we could see someone on deck point toward us. It was Dutch's wife, Joyce, and Barbara.

Pap kicked the *Vanguard* out of gear fifty yards from us, and I ran up to the lee side, waiting until the swell was just right, and darted in to let Dutch off. Barb and Joyce grabbed him and I backed away and waited. When we came in the next time, Duke handed up our furs and rifles, then our bed rolls. And at last he and I climbed painfully aboard, stiff and half frozen, icicles hanging from our beards.

I tied the skiff line to the stern cleat, and Pap put the clutch into gear and headed home. A little later Barb and Joyce were pushing mugs of steaming coffee into our numb hands, and Pap told us he'd been unable to get the *Vanguard* started yesterday because of the cold weather, and had run the batteries down. This morning, after charging them all night, he'd finally got the engine going.

11

Ordeal

"I'm afraid you boys have picked an unscrupulous fur buyer," Pap said that night. We had all taken baths and shaved, and now with our stomachs full, we sat with our wives around Ma's big table and listened to the sad news.

"When I shipped the first batch of furs by air mail, I told your friend O'Callahan to wire back an offer." Pap rose and went to the hutch across the room. He brought back two yellow telegrams and handed one to me.

> AM HOLDING YOUR FURS TO BE AUCTIONED AT THE FUR EXCHANGE STOP WILL ENDEAVOR TO GET YOU HIGHEST POSSIBLE PRICE STOP
> B. J. O'CALLAHAN

"Well, I'll be——!" I said, and passed it to Duke.

When Dutch had read it, Pap went on: "I plainly saw we had a sly one to contend with. I checked over his letter and brochure and saw that he had professed to be a legitimate fur buyer, paying cash for the furs that were shipped to him."

"And now, instead of making us an offer, he wants

Ordeal

to hold the furs and charge us a commission for selling them—possibly for less than we might get on the open market now!" Duke said.

"Exactly," Pap said. "I sent him another wire to make a cash offer immediately—or air mail the furs back to us collect." Pap showed us the answering wire that had come over the radiophone via the A. C. S. station in Juneau.

PLEASE AIR MAIL ME THE REST OF YOUR FURS IMMEDIATELY STOP WILL THEN MAKE OFFER STOP

B. J. O'CALLAHAN

Duke grinned. "O'Callahan sure isn't short on guts, is he?"

"What are we going to do?" Dutch asked.

"We're at a distinct disadvantage," I said finally, after giving it some thought. "For one thing, we've lost two weeks' time with this storm; now, if we decide to send the rest of our furs to one of the reputable buyers like Goldberg or Maas Stephens in St. Louis, we'll be late getting them down there—and still might have trouble getting our furs back from friend O'Callahan. There's only one thing to do, as I see it."

"One of us fly down to Seattle and jerk those furs out from under this joker," Duke said.

"Precisely."

Pap nodded. "The sooner the better. He could have already peddled the furs, and you might have a time getting your money."

"We'll get the furs back from him," I said, "and we'll have a good-sized batch to show one of the other buyers. We'll be there personally to bargain with them and make a better deal. What's your tally, Dutch?"

Dutch took his tally book from his shirt pocket. "Well, altogether—counting the ones O'Callahan has—we've got three hundred sixty-two mink, and forty-six otter pelts."

"Who's going?" Pap asked.

"Let's flip," I said.

"Count me out," Dutch said, "I've seen all I want of the bright lights for quite a while. Besides, I almost got run over by a car in Juneau when Joyce and I were married."

"You and me, then," Duke said, finding a coin. "Heads you go—tails me." He flipped the coin into the air, caught it, and snapped it onto the back of his hand.

"Tails—you go," I said.

The following day dawned late, and a heavy snowstorm obscured Warm Springs Bay. Duke called Alaska Coastal Airlines in Juneau and requested a plane to pick him up if the visibility improved during the day.

We got all of our furs together and graded them into separate piles, then wrapped them in clean burlap sacks, and our wives sewed the seams together. The burlap would let them "breathe," and they would not mold.

In the afternoon the snowstorm eased off, and visibility improved enough so the seaplane could fly. At two P.M. it landed in the bay and taxied up to the airplane float.

Duke, dressed in a wool whipcord cruiser outfit (commonly called an "Alaskan tuxedo"), kissed his wife of two and a half months good-by, climbed into the passenger compartment of the plane and took a seat beside the only other passenger, an elderly man from

Ordeal

Tenakee. The plane was an ancient Lockheed Vega, similar to the one Will Rogers and Wiley Post had been killed in many years before. We handed the bundles of furs up to Duke, wished him luck and shut the door.

A moment later the pilot, sitting alone in the forward compartment, started the engine and taxied away from the float. Then with a full-throated roar of the engine, the plane began to pick up speed. Presently the pontoons were up on top of the water, and then it was airborne. It quickly gained altitude, a mere speck against the snowy mountains, and then was lost from sight. . . .

At five A.M. a knock at our cabin door awoke Barb and me. I slipped into a shirt and pair of pants and went to answer it. Ma stood there with a look of incalculable grief on her face.

"What is it, Ma?" I asked gently.

"Duke . . . he was . . . " she stopped, unable to go on.

I brought her inside and she sat down, crying now. "The plane crashed after it left here . . . " she said at last. "He's dead."

I pulled on my boots and jacket, and leaving her with Barb, stepped outside.

Fine snow was falling, slanting ahead of a light breeze from the east. I stood there in front of the cabin in shock. I could not believe it. Just this afternoon. . . .

I pulled myself together and went across the walk to Dutch's cabin and awoke him. When he had dressed we headed for Pap's house.

Pap was sitting at the table, deep lines etching his face. Across the table sat David John, a Thlinget Indian from the village of Angoon, to the north. He was a tall, good-looking man in his thirties. David owned a seine boat named *St. John,* and he fished in the summer months and trapped or hunted seals during the winters.

"Hello, David," I said.

"Hi, Wayne . . . Dutch," he said to us, uncomfortable in the way people are when they bring such tragic news.

I went to the stove and made a pot of coffee, and when it was finished, poured David a cup.

"What happened, David?" I asked at last.

"I been hunting seals in Kelp Bay," David said, sugaring his coffee. "Last night I'm anchored up in God's Pocket and at nine o'clock I hear the news from Juneau. Radio man say Alaska Coastal plane crash on mountain on south side of Tenakee Inlet. He say that another plane from Juneau fly over wreckage just before dark. Plane crash in forest—nothing left but little pieces of that plane. They don't see how nobody live through that." David paused, sipping his coffee. "I'm hunting seals in Kelp Bay. I remember when that plane fly over, maybe two-thirty. Looks like it comes from Warm Springs Bay. After I hear about crash on radio, I say, 'David, better you pull up anchor and run to Warm Springs Bay—maybe one of your friends on that plane!' "

There was nothing for us to say. I went over to the radiophone and switched the receiver on. As I stood there listening to the crackle of static, I sipped my coffee absently, and thought of Duke. . . .

Billy Dean Short . . . as a little boy of six, he had been given an old collapsible top hat by a neighbor. He had folded pieces of newspaper and put them inside the

Ordeal

sweatband until it fitted him, then had worn it around at a jaunty angle. Pap promptly nicknamed him "The Duke"—and he'd been Duke ever since. We had been living in Colorado then, and shortly afterwards he fell beneath a wagon with several tons of potatoes on it. One of the wheels ran over his right thigh, and later he developed osteomyelitis in the ball joint of his hip. He had spent several miserable years in a body cast, several more on crutches, but he had never lost his easy grin, nor had he complained. His right leg was an inch and a half shorter than the left, and because of it, he had a chronic curvature of the spine. His back and leg pained him constantly, but he had hunted and trapped and stayed right up with Dutch and me without ever a word of complaint—and now he was dead. . . .

As I stood there in front of the radiophone, we heard a Coast Guard cutter reporting to Juneau. Their position was off East Point at the entrance to Tenakee Inlet. When they had signed off with Juneau, I called them and found out they had been dispatched with corpsmen and a rescue team to hike to the scene of the crash. They also informed me that a party of Indians had left Tenakee Springs shortly after the plane had gone down. If we would stand by the Coast Guard frequency, they should have a report from the Indians shortly after daylight.

We waited silently for them to call back. Barb, Joyce and Ma came in, and we told them what we had learned.

"Do you think we should wake Shirley—and tell her?" Ma asked.

"Let's wait until we hear from the cutter," Pap said.

Daylight slowly crept across the land, and still we waited silently for the call.

— *THIS RAW LAND* —

"KWB 36, Baranof," the cutter's call boomed through the silence. I jumped up and went to the set and told them to go ahead.

"One of our men has just returned from the scene of the crash. The pilot is dead, but the two passengers, though badly injured, are alive. They are being carried down off the mountains in stretchers now, and should be here in another half-hour. We have Doctor Carter aboard the cutter, and as soon as they come aboard, we'll get underway for Juneau."

I stood there dumbly a long moment, then finally thanked the man and turned to the others. The Duke was alive!

Barb and Joyce went out into the new day and crossed to Shirley's cabin to somehow tell her what had happened. . . .

"Here is the way things are now," Doctor Carter said to Shirley, Dutch and me. We had flown into Juneau late that afternoon, and now stood before him in a corridor in St. Ann's Hospital. "He's lucky to be alive at all. Severe head injuries, upper teeth all broken off, his body a solid mass of bruises and torn muscles. I spent four hours this afternoon operating on his left leg. Had a heck of a time fitting all the broken bone back—have a plate and screws holding it together, and a leg cast on now. We're still taking tests and X-rays, so we don't know what internal injuries he has. We'll just have to wait and see . . . "

"If he isn't hurt too badly inside, what does the future look like for him?" I asked.

Carter thought it over a moment, then said: "He has

Ordeal

that short right leg, now the left one all broken to hell—frankly, I think his working days are over."

"May we see him?" Shirley asked.

Carter nodded and led us down the corridor to his room.

Duke lay there sleeping off the anesthetic, so battered and covered with bandages that we hardly recognized him. The next night when we went into his room we found the old Duke, a little subdued perhaps, but coherent. Before the nurses ran us off, he told us about the plane crash. . . .

They had been bucking strong head winds after leaving Warm Springs Bay, but everything had gone fine until just before they got to Tenakee Inlet. Coming across the south end of Chichagof Island, the pilot kept climbing to clear the mountain peaks, one of which reached to four thousand feet. As they started to drop down the far side into Tenakee Inlet, the motor coughed a couple of times.

The other passenger, an older man, was sitting across the aisle from Duke. "Sure hope we're not out of gas," he said in a joking manner.

"Me, too," Duke said, not really concerned.

The engine coughed again, then abruptly stopped. A moment later it started with a roar, and the plane began to lift again. The pilot, riding the "death" seat in the nose just behind the engine compartment, made a motion with his arm, and Duke unbuckled his seat belt and went to the small glass port that separated them. The pilot was saying something but Duke couldn't make out his words. The engine stopped again and the pilot turned frantically back to his controls as the plane immediately began to settle down. Duke went back to his seat and buckled himself in. He didn't know much about airplanes, but he knew enough about engines to realize that they were indeed out of gasoline.

The pilot choked the engine; it would pick up and lift them up a few feet, then they would begin to settle again. Duke looked out of his window and saw that it was several miles to the inlet. There was not a chance to make the water, he knew, and there were no muskegs to crash-land on—only the dense forest.

"We're going to crash," Duke said to the old man across the aisle, watching the tops of the trees only fifty feet below the wings now.

The engine was dead, and the treetops were nearer. Duke watched in fascination as the trees came closer and closer, until they were eating away the wings. It would not be long now.

Suddenly there was a blinding flash of lightning and a film of red covered his eyes. . . .

Gnawing dreams, peculiar little creatures pulling at him, trying to tell him that he might freeze to death if he wasn't careful. Now they were gone and the red haze was back, blinding him. He forced himself back into reality, blinked the red film away and looked out upon a surrealistic world: he was in a sitting position in the woods and about him was scattered some sort of wreckage. He was all alone. When he tried to move, the pain hit him like the thrust of a sharp knife. . . .

When he regained consciousness, he began to gag, then vomited. Through the red film he peered into the snow beside him and saw a mass of blood and broken teeth. Then he remembered the plane, and the trees getting closer and closer. . . .

I must be hurt bad, he thought. Then: *But, by God, I'm alive!*

He spit out more blood, and became determined to learn something of his injuries.

There was no feeling on the left side of his body, but he was able to wiggle the fingers of his right hand; then he lifted his arm and put his fingers to his eyes. They came away bloody. He wiped the blood away, and for the first time began to really see about him. His right leg was stretched out in front of him. Across the left leg was one of the plane's pontoons.

Duke felt for the pack of cigarettes he carried in a shirt pocket—miraculously, they were still there. He fed one into his battered mouth, worked his lighter out of a pocket of his trousers, and lit up, trying to form some sort of a plan of action.

He was sitting on a little knoll which dropped off to a creek below. He couldn't see the creek, but he could hear it. There was a trail of wreckage leading over the knoll, and he felt sure the pilot was down there. He took the cigarette out of his mouth and tried to yell, but the guttural noise that came from his lips sounded more animal than human.

"Has anyone fed the cats?" a voice answered him.

Duke turned his head and saw the old man stumbling along with a dazed look. He was cut badly around the head, and one of his arms hung limply at his side.

"Hey!" Duke cried hoarsely. "Come help me get this pontoon off my leg!"

— THIS RAW LAND —

"I've got to get home," the old man said, shaking his head. "I don't think anyone has fed the cats," and he wandered off into the forest.

Duke began painfully working debris out from under the pontoon. Twenty minutes later he was able to free his left leg, but he was sickened when he saw it: the ankle was so badly crushed that the foot had turned 180 degrees with the toes pointed straight down. He lay back to let the sick feeling pass, then lit another cigarette. The hope of making his way out to the beach was gone now.

He sat up again and worked his belt from around his waist. Using a flat piece of wood from the wrecked plane, he laid it alongside the crushed ankle for a splint, then laboriously wound the belt tightly around with his right hand, and buckled it.

Duke called to the pilot on the other side of the little knoll, but the only answer he got was the soft sigh of the wind through the treetops. Then across the creek there came the shriek of an eagle as dusk began to settle over the forest.

He counted his cigarettes and found there were ten left. I'll smoke one every two hours, he said to himself. He lay there, as close to death as he had ever been, and took account of his life: twenty-seven years old, married to Shirley just two and a half months, and just last night she had told him she thought she was pregnant. He thought of the son or daughter he would never see, and suddenly vowed he would stay alive somehow!

The sound of a plane came, faint at first, then louder by degrees, until it roared overhead. It was a Grumman "Goose" and it soon passed from sight. Presently it was back overhead. Duke was sure it had spotted the slash

Ordeal

in the forest where they had crashed. He felt a lot better. All he had to do now was to somehow live through the night until a rescue party could get through at daylight. The sound of the plane gradually faded away into the north. It was almost dark, and he pulled his coat tighter around him and tried to ease into a more comfortable position.

The wind had died and it began to clear overhead. The sky changed to a pale, icy blue, and presently the stars came out. Every now and then he spit out blood, but he didn't know if it was due to internal injuries or merely his gums bleeding from the broken teeth. It was strange; if he didn't try to move there was really not much pain. *I must be hurt pretty bad if I can't feel any more than this,* he thought.

It was dark now. He lit another cigarette, worrying about the pilot, thinking he should have tried to make it down there . . . and he wondered where the old man was.

There followed a long, confused, nightmarish period filled with things that happened in the past, snatches of conversations long forgotten, surrealistic images.

Later he became aware of faint voices and he could not figure out if they were real or imaginary. He lit another cigarette, then held the flame of the lighter over the watch on the wrist of his dead left hand. It was one o'clock. Then he heard the voices again, off to his right.

"We'll never find them until daylight," a man said.

Duke sat up and tried to yell, but only a strangled sound came out. He lit the cigarette lighter and looked around him. A couple of feet away was a stick and he took it and began to beat upon the aluminum pontoon.

A little later he saw the flash of a lantern through the trees.

It was four Indians from Tenakee. They came up to Duke and squatted down in the snow beside him. "You okay?" one asked.

"I'm okay," Duke said, "but I think the pilot is down there toward the creek, and the other passenger is an old fellow—he's wandering around here somewhere—kinda out of his head."

Two of them took a lantern and went down toward the creek. A few minutes later they were back. "He's down there all right, with the engine—but he's dead. Got a limb through his chest," one of them said. Then they began looking for the old man.

The two men with Duke looked him over, and he saw the horror in their faces.

"Lord God! I hope I don't look that bad!" Duke said.

"You don't look so mighty fine, partner," one of the Indians said, trying to smile. "I don't think we better move you. We'll clear a place in the snow and build a fire."

The other man opened his pack and took out several blankets. He spread them over Duke and tucked them around him. He folded another one and put it beneath Duke's head. "How about a cup of coffee?" he asked, breaking out a thermos.

The fire was going now, and the steaming coffee warmed Duke. "How'd you find us so soon?" he asked.

"We were standing in Dermit O'Toole's office in Tenakee when we heard the pilot call Juneau and tell them he was out of gas, and going to crash. He gave his position—and that was the last we heard. Dermit gave us

Ordeal

a medical kit, some blankets, thermos of coffee and soup —and we borrowed a skiff and outboard motor and crossed the inlet."

"You hurting pretty bad?" the other man asked.

"I can make it fine," Duke said, glad that he was not alone.

"Well, I got morphine," the man said, "but I don't know too much about using it. I remember in Korea the medics didn't like to use it if a man had a bad head wound." He held the lantern close and studied Duke's head. "You got some pretty deep cuts, but they're not bleeding now."

Soon the other two Indians came back with the old man. They got him to sit down by the fire and wrapped a blanket around him.

"You sure they fed the cats?" he asked anxiously, sipping the coffee they put in his hands.

"We went over to your place and fed them just a little while ago," one of the men said gently.

"Well . . . I thought maybe no one thought to feed them . . ." he said, pacified now.

"A Coast Guard cutter is on its way out from Juneau —should be getting into the inlet soon," said one of the men. "They have Doc Carter aboard. As soon as it begins to get a little light, two of us will follow the creek down to the beach and guide the rescue team in."

"Fine," Duke said, and drifted off into his own nightmarish world.

The Coast Guard rescue party arrived shortly after daylight with two corpsmen and three stretchers. They eased Duke up onto one of the stretchers and covered him with blankets. Then, with the old fellow and dead pilot in the other two, they started down the mountain toward the waiting Cost Guard cutter.

"Hey, I forgot about our furs!" Duke said to one of the Coast Guardsmen when they stopped to rest.

"Some of our men are back there looking for the mail bags—they'll find them."

Duke nodded, satisfied, and the men put out their cigarettes and picked up his stretcher again. It felt mighty good to be alive at all. He made a vow that if he pulled through he'd take a little closer look at life in general. . . .

Two days later I was in Seattle with our furs, ready to take on O'Callahan. Astute as he was, the owl-eyed little pseudo-Irishman was no match for my fury. I reasoned that O'Callahan was indirectly responsible for Duke lying in his hospital bed, possibly crippled for life.

I had first gone to three other fur buyers and shown them the furs I had brought down, and received offers for them. Now I went into O'Callahan's unimpressive hole in the wall near the waterfront, introduced myself, and laying a .357 Magnum pistol on the counter, announced that he had ten minutes to trot out our furs— or I would personally gut shoot him. Pointedly looking at his quivering *pauncho grande,* I observed that even a poor pistol shot such as myself would hardly miss it.

I had just bought the pistol down the street at Warshall's Sporting Supply. It was not loaded, of course, but O'Callahan could not know this. His dark eyes began to fill with tears as he told me how tough it was for a poor boy from New York to break into the fur-buying business. One of his sons had been born with a club foot and a hare-

Ordeal

lip—and God only knew what the cost of the operations would be. On top of this his mother-in-law—whom he also supported—had a rare, incurable cancer and——

I interrupted him before he had me crying, countering with the details of Duke's plane crash.

O'Callahan began to see that this wild-eyed trapper from the far north was not to be taken in by his sad stories, and quite possibly—in view of the big pistol on the counter—might be dangerous.

I saw a look of anguish on his face then. "You've already sold our furs, haven't you?" I demanded loudly, pounding the counter.

O'Callahan looked at the floor, nodding silently.

"All right," I said, "I want seventeen dollars a pelt for the mink, and twenty-eight dollars for the otter." This was two dollars a pelt more than the best offer I'd received from the other fur buyers.

O'Callahan cried that it would break him, but nevertheless he dug out our shipping slip, began to punch on an adding machine, and presently wrote out a check for the total amount.

He pushed the check across the counter with a beaten look, although I knew he had still made a fair profit on the furs. I put the check into my shirt pocket, then picked up the pistol, which had already paid for itself, and shoved it beneath my belt. I buttoned my overcoat over the butt and looked at O'Callahan.

"Let's you and I walk down the street to the bank," I said to him.

Twenty minutes later I pocketed the cash and left him standing dejectedly on the curb in front of the bank.

"So long, O'Callahan," I said, and walked off into the crowd.

But O'Callahan was not one to hold a grudge. Moreover, he had all the innate qualities it took to be a successful fur buyer. The next winter we received his brochure again, with predictions of high fur prices, and he sent a letter informing me of the personal crises that continued to plague him, ending it with the sincere hope that Duke was up and about and in shape to trap again. His letter implied there were no hard feel:ngs on his part because of our past differences, and he would be delighted to handle our furs in an impeccable manner in the future. . . .

12

The Frontier Wife

During the summer months we had been constantly on the move as we chased the elusive salmon; there had been different sights to see every day, new faces as we met other fishermen and their wives. In fact, it had been one long, fascinating vacation for Barb. Now, after my return from Seattle, Barb was concentrating on becoming an efficient frontier wife, and she was experiencing some frustration.

There were no nearby supermarkets or shopping centers as she had been accustomed to, no theaters, night clubs or restaurants to break the monotony. Anything she might need to keep her household running must come on the mailboat, *Yakobi*, which left Juneau weekly, weather permitting, and made the arduous 500-mile circuit of the outlying district. Foodstuffs must be ordered from town weeks in advance. Clothing and household goods came from Seattle via the mail-order catalogues. During the winter months we saw few travelers, and our social life was limited to dinner or card games with the other members of the family.

People living in such isolation must be able to entertain themselves, especially in the winters when the days are short and the nights so long, when the savage wind howls days on end and the snow swirls outside your cabin and the drifts get deeper and deeper. My family, perhaps from necessity, were all omnivorous readers, and each of us had hobbies. Pap was forever building something; Ma knitted heavy wool sweaters and mittens from English yarn for all the members of the family; Dutch was interested in photography, among other things; Duke was a gun crank, making rifles and checkering fancy inlaid stocks. One of my spare-time projects was writing. I had always had a desire to put words on paper, and spent much of my spare time studying books on writing techniques and turning out short stories that, considering the distance to New York, seemed to return (rejection slips attached) with amazing speed and regularity.

Barb, like my brothers' wives, had her hands full just trying to adapt to our way of life. One of the things that gave her more trouble than anything else was baking. She was a fair cook, but like many of her sisters of this generation, she had been dependent upon the corner bakery and the supermarket's array of frozen or packaged biscuits, buns and pastries. Now she was trying to learn to mix up a batch of biscuits or lightbread from scratch, as my mother did, and some of her attempts were atrocious. The infuriating part of it was that, after baking

The Frontier Wife

for a good many years, I was a pretty fair dough artist myself, and I could not always keep my opinion of her latest effort to myself. This inevitably led to trouble.

Another thing that was hard for Barb to get used to was my absence much of the time on hunting, trapping or fishing trips. For many years Ma had worried about us, and now Barb, shore bound because of her pregnancy, complained whenever I got ready to take off on a trip. I tried to explain that this was where our livelihood came from and that, generally speaking, my chances were probably a lot better than if I were a city man driving the freeways to and from work. Moreover, I emphasized, this was the only life I seemed suited for—so she had better get adjusted to my being away a great deal of the time. But after our near-disastrous trip from Surprise Harbor in the skiff, then Duke's plane crash, she was far from being reassured.

But as the winter progressed Barb became more and more preoccupied with thoughts of the baby she was carrying, and by the time our first son was born in the spring, she had grown used to my coming and going. Mark, two months premature, came unexpectedly while I was away on a fishing trip in May. Ma was able to call out a plane from Juneau by radiophone, and Barb arrived at the hospital only a few minutes before the little fellow was born, weighing a scant three and a half pounds. By the time word was relayed from boat to boat and caught up with me on the fishing grounds—it was all over.

In the months that followed, Barb was forced to cope with the many problems that arose while I was away, and she had little time to be bored. One evening when Mark was just beginning to walk, a huge brownie with a yearling cub strolled into the front yard where the little fellow was playing. Barb grabbed one of my rifles from the rack by the door, jacked a cartridge into the chamber, then slipped quietly out to scoop up Mark and return slowly to the safety of the house under the malevolent eye of the big she-bear.

This was some transformation from a city girl who, such a short time ago, had been terrified by the cry of a loon. Moreover, in a surprisingly short time she was efficiently keeping a home and a garden in a country that contributed little to domestic comfort—and she enjoyed it.

In the spring of 1957, I accepted a job running a cannery tender out of Icy Inlet, to the north, and Barb, after being left on the beach for more than two years, suggested I take her and little Mark along as the crew. So we began packing....

PART THREE

13

The Fish Buyers

The *Apex I* lay at the Northern Commercial Company's float in Juneau, a derelict from another era. Originally she had been a tender for the old Apex Mine on Chichagof Island, and the ravages of time and prolonged disuse lay heavily upon her. The old-style pilothouse stood ramrod straight with never an inch of rake to relieve its uncompromising lines. To top it all she was painted a fire-engine red. She was forty-eight feet in length with twelve feet of beam, and carved into her hatch-combing timber were numerals indicating that she had a hold capacity of sixteen tons.

Barb, Mark and I stood on the float looking at our new home.

"Boat?" Mark asked, pointing a stubby forefinger at the vessel.

"If you could call it that," I said in disgust, and lifted him on deck. I gave Barb a hand to help her aboard, wondering how in blazes I had let the Supreme Commander talk me into this deal. . . .

— THIS RAW LAND —

It had happened in a roundabout manner. The indomitable Duke, after two years and several operations, had gone back skippering a cannery tender for Norman Holm, who, with his fleet of tenders, had a contract with Pacific American Fisheries to buy and pack seine and gill-net fish to their cannery in Icy Strait. Norman, whom we called the "Supreme Commander," had offered me a unique deal this spring: he would turn the *Apex I* over to me, supply everything except our food, and pay me one cent a pound for all the gill-net fish that I bought in Port Snettisham, regardless of who delivered them to the cannery. This meant that if there was a big salmon run in Port Snettisham and other tenders had to be dispatched to help me pack fish—I would *still* receive one cent a pound on all the fish these tenders delivered to the cannery.

Barb and I had talked it over and decided the two of us could handle the job, thus saving the money I would have to pay a deck hand. We were gambling, but if there was a big run of fish this season we had a chance to make a pile of money.

Now we stood on deck looking at *Apex I*. I had known it was an old boat, but I wasn't prepared for the sight that met our eyes. There was nothing to do, however, but dig in and try to get her into some kind of order.

The galley was situated in the after part of the pilothouse, and along one wall was an oil-burning range, a counter and sink, cupboards, and a table with built-in benches that served as storage for canned goods. A trap door in the deck gave access to the engine room below, as well as to the sleeping quarters in the fo'c'sle. I started a fire in the range and put water on to heat, then went down to take a look at the ancient engine.

The Fish Buyers

In a day when vessels of this size invariably had diesels, *Apex I* still had an immense gasoline engine with a four-to-one reduction gear. While Barb scrubbed down the galley and began to get things shipshape, I broke out my tool box and went to work. . . .

A week later *Apex I* was a completely different vessel. The galley had been scrubbed and freshly painted; the cast-iron stove gone over with steel wool and a coat of stove black; the sleeping quarters in the fo'c'sle had been painted and outfitted with new mattresses. I had tuned up the engine and changed the oil, as well as scraped the hull and painted it black. The glaring red of the pilothouse was now a sedate white, and we were ready to move our personal gear out of the Gastineau Hotel and stow it aboard.

Barb and I had been concerned about Mark, for a two-year-old is difficult to keep corralled, especially on a boat. Finally we solved the problem: I found a piece of heavy netting in the lazarette, bound the edges with rope, then secured one edge to the bottom of his bunk; while he slept we could hook the top edge of the netting to the top of his bunk cubicle, and he would not fall out as the boat rolled. I also bought a highchair, drilled holes in the back and the legs and bolted it to one wall in the galley. We were proud of our ingenuity, and it was to work out very well.

The gill-net season for sockeye salmon opened on the fifth of July, and that morning I went to the bank and cashed a $20,000 buying fund check that the Supreme Commander had given me. I had groceries delivered to the boat, then moved over to the oil dock to take on fuel and water. In the afternoon we took four tons of ground ice into the hold at the cold-storage dock. We were all

— *THIS RAW LAND* —

ready then, and cut loose the lines and headed out the channel, our destination Port Snettisham.

Port Snettisham lies thirty-odd miles southeast of Juneau on the mainland shore. The entrance was perhaps three miles wide and five miles long, then it opened into two arms; one arm ran about seventeen miles northward where the Speel River emptied into its head, and the short south arm received the waters of the Whiting River. Off of these rivers were several fresh-water lakes, and in these lakes the sockeye salmon returned from their three-year voyage on the high seas to spawn and, like the other four species, die.

Around nine o'clock that evening we entered the mouth of Port Snettisham and ran up the center of the inlet, twisting and turning among the many boats whose gill nets were stretched across the inlet. The gill nets were 150 fathoms long, three deep, with leads spaced along the bottom to hold the net down, and corks along the top to float it. The mesh of the net was of a size that when the incoming fish ran into it in the murky river water, they were caught by their gill covers.

The fishermen had large power-driven reels in the after part of their boats, and they let their nets out over rollers mounted on the stern, and drifted. Every now and then they reeled the net in, picking the sockeye out of the net as it came aboard.

The gill netters were limited to fishing three days a week; the remaining four days permitted a certain percentage of fish to enter the lakes and spawn. We would buy their catches each day and ice them down in the hold. Then, at the end of the three-day fishing period, we would run our load to the cannery in Icy Inlet to be canned.

The Fish Buyers

Gill-net fish have stopped feeding by the time they enter the inlets, so it is not necessary to dress them, and they are bought, as we say, "in the round."

As we worked our way through the boats and nets toward the anchorage in the south arm, I counted some eighty boats fishing. Some were big new boats with all the latest equipment, others were merely oversized skiffs which were powered by outboard motors, and the fishermen pulled their nets in by sheer brute strength.

It was almost eleven o'clock before I got the anchor down, and dusk was fast coming to the land. I shut the engine off, dropped anchor, and while Barb fixed supper, I set up the platform scales on the back deck in such a manner that I could trip the big metal box and send the fish sliding into the hold after they had been weighed. Finally I had it set up to my satisfaction and we ate.

After supper Barb put Mark to bed and we carried our cups of coffee outside and sat down on the hatch. The mountains rose all around us, some to over six thousand feet. A loon's haunting cry came, then the gentle sound of a seal's breath being expelled as it surfaced fifty yards from the boat and studied us.

"Beautiful country," Barb said, and I nodded assent.

The following morning we were up by four o'clock, ate, and pulled the anchor. My plan was to begin picking up fish off the Whiting River and continue along the eastern shore of the inlet until I had serviced all the boats in that area. Then I would come back down the western shore, turn into the mouth of the entrance, cross to the southern side and work back toward the anchorage by evening.

When I came to the first boat I eased the *Apex I*

alongside, while he still hung off one end of his net. We made our lines fast, and I handed him a "pue." The pue is much like a pitchfork, but has only one tine. The fisherman stuck the tine into the heads of his fish and pitched them one by one onto the deck of the *Apex I*.

The five species of salmon return to spawn in this order: the king salmon in early spring, the sockeye in July, followed by the humpbacks, cohos and dogs (so called because of their long dog-like teeth). Although this was the sockeye season, there was always a sprinkling of early humpies, cohos and dogs. Since the price per pound varied on each species, I weighed them separately, calling out the weights to Barb in the galley, before dumping them into the hold.

By the time the fish were weighed and the fisherman had washed his deck down, Barb had his fish ticket made out and stepped on deck to pay him in cash for his catch. Then I handed him a cold beer, untied and headed for the next boat. This was repeated until we had serviced all the boats and returned to the anchorage for the night. Then, as Barb began supper, I climbed down into the hold and iced the fish.

We had been concerned about how little Mark would fit into such a life, but now we saw there was no reason to worry. He was quite happy with it all. In good weather he wore his life jacket and played on deck, and when it rained he was content to pass the time in the galley with his toys.

At the end of the three-day fishing period we had bought a little over 10,000 pounds of fish. I was very disappointed as we left Port Snettisham and headed for the cannery, roughly a hundred-mile run. By the time

The Fish Buyers

we took our groceries out of our commissions we would make about seventy-five dollars for the week.

"Maybe it will get better," Barb said.

"I hope so."

At the cannery we tied alongside the fish elevator, and the Filipino unloading crew came aboard and began to pitch the salmon out of the hold and into the elevator which carried them up into the cannery. When we were unloaded I washed down the hold and we moved over to the main float where we tied alongside Duke's *Hannah C*.

That evening, after taking advantage of the cannery's washroom and showers, we all got together for supper in the spacious galley of the *Hannah C*, and I introduced everyone to Barb.

Jim Brown—middle thirties, dark-complexioned, ex-gambler, bartender, cab driver, Texan—was skipper of the *Rio De Oro*, and serviced the Taku Inlet, which was just north of Port Snettisham.

His wife, Betty—a stunning brunette in toreador pants—seemed starkly out of place on a tender.

Bob Horchover—soft-spoken, good-looking man in his twenties—was skipper of the *Theo E*, and was servicing Portland Canal, three hundred miles south on the Alaskan-Canadian border. Bob attended dental college in Seattle during the winters.

Linnie Bardason—flaxen-haired, six-foot-seven giant of Icelandic extraction—was skipper of the *Neptune*, and serviced Chilkat Inlet, to the north. Linnie had been a tender captain since his late teens. During the winters in Seattle, he took college extension courses in business administration.

Norman Holm—thirty-six years old, averaged-sized,

Harvard man, ex-naval officer, fisherman, promoter *par excellence*, owner of the five tenders, whom we called the Supreme Commander.

The introductions over, Barb and Betty Brown began to fry steaks while the rest of us gathered around a bottle of bourbon the Supreme Commander had brought with him—and talked fishing.

The next morning we left for Juneau, to take on fuel, groceries and ice, then returned to Port Snettisham.

By the end of the sockeye season our hopes of making any money looked poor. The run of humpback salmon hadn't amounted to much yet, and Holm decided to pull the *Rio De Oro* off Taku Inlet and sent Brown to Portland Canal to help the *Theo E*, which was swamped by a sudden run of fish. We were to service the Taku Inlet fishermen in conjunction with our Snettisham operation. This made it doubly hard, for after picking up fish all day in Snettisham, we had to run up Stephen's Passage to Taku Inlet and take care of the boats there. Even though the fishermen were hardly getting enough salmon to eat, we still had to go through the motions and check every boat.

One day in early September we were heading back to the fishing grounds after delivering the past week's fish, and I turned on the radiophone to hear one of the gill netters calling me. I answered, and learned that a big run of dog salmon had hit Port Snettisham and Taku Inlet simultaneously. All the boats were swamp-loaded and screaming for a tender, the fisherman said.

I opened the throttle another notch and looked at Barb. "This is what we've been waiting for."

"I hope so," she said.

The Fish Buyers

As we steamed into the mouth of Port Snettisham, some of the gill netters began to reel their nets aboard and run toward us; all were sunk low in the water. They wanted to unload their fish and get their nets back into the water. I slowed down and drifted as the first two came alongside. While I weighed up one boat's fish and Barb paid the fisherman, the man on the other side was pitching his catch aboard. By that time another boat had taken the first one's place and the salmon were beginning to pile up in the fish hold.

We worked steadily all night, and by dawn we had 28,000 pounds aboard; we had serviced every boat. As we ran up Stephen's Passage toward the Taku River, I ate breakfast and sat at the galley table sipping coffee and resting while Barb took the wheel. I knew we could take only a portion of the fish that were waiting for us at Taku, so I called Juneau on the radiophone and finally located Norman Holm. I told him about the run of fish that was beginning to hit Snettisham and Taku, and asked for another tender to replace us. Holm said none were available, but he would try to charter another vessel. I was to take all the fish I could pack and head for the cannery. We would keep in touch by phone.

As we entered Taku Inlet, boats were waiting for us, and by the time the *Apex I* lost steerage way, they swarmed alongside, tying six deep on either side. Then the fish began to come aboard.

The problem now confronting me was this: would the rotten old hull stay afloat? Lord only knew how long it had been since she had carried a full load, and already she was making enough water to keep one power-driven bilge pump running steadily.

Hour after hour the fish continued to come aboard, and still the boats came. The hold was completely full, and I was wading knee-deep through fish as I continued to buy. The stern was down, and the sea ran over the well deck. Finally I yelled to the fishermen alongside and told them I couldn't take any more, but they paid no attention to me and continued to pitch fish aboard.

In desperation I began pitching fish up on the foredeck, but at last I knew I must go; the old girl was terribly overloaded now.

I threw down my pue, and told the boats alongside I was through buying, to untie their lines and wait for another tender. But after all the previous poor fishing, they were determined to get their fish sold and get back on the grounds to catch more.

"Dammit!" I yelled, "Can't you see we're loaded—that we're near sinking now!"

They stared unblinkingly at me with bloodshot eyes, and continued to pitch their fish aboard.

I stepped into the galley to face Barb. "What's wrong with them?" she asked in alarm.

"They've been fishing hard for thirty straight hours and they're not thinking right. All that's in their minds is to unload so they can get back to fishing. Put the engine in forward," I said, and grabbed a butcher knife from the rack behind the stove. I stepped out on deck and began chopping loose their lines. Curses greeted my actions, but I had no intention of arguing. "Give it some throttle!" I called to Barb, and the *Apex I* moved sluggishly from between the boats.

"That's just like the big companies!" one man yelled.

The Fish Buyers

"They cry for fish, and when you bring 'em—they won't buy 'em!"

"What in the hell are we going to do?" another cried desperately.

"There's another tender on the way!" I yelled back, then went into the wheelhouse to take the wheel from Barb. I opened the throttle and we moved out into Stephen's Passage.

Barb handed me a cup of coffee and I perched my weary frame on a stool in front of the wheel. The two of us had already put in thirty solid hours, and with the slow time we were making with this load, we could look forward to another eleven hours before we got to the cannery. I was glad of one thing, however: the sea was calm, and the weather forecast good.

I switched the radiophone onto the cannery frequency and gave them a call, telling them we were headed in with a full load, and asked if Holm had another tender on the way.

As far as they knew he had been unable to charter one, but he was still in Juneau trying to find one. Duke, diverted to help the *Rio De Oro*, was on his way up from Portland Canal with a 110,000-pound load, and would be available as soon as he was unloaded, but that would not be until two days later.

I left on the radiophone in case anyone called, and Barb fixed something to eat. She took the wheel while I ate, then I lit a cigar and took over again. When Barb and Mark had finished eating I talked her into going below and lying down. Mark and I stood our wheel watch, talking and sometimes singing together to keep me from falling asleep. Weariness was heavy upon me and the idleness of a wheel watch was pure misery. Once I fell completely asleep as I stood before the wheel, and my knees buckled and I went down before awakening.

At nine o'clock, I carried Mark down to his bunk and put him in, then tied up the web gate so he could not fall out. I went back to the wheelhouse again and continued to fight off my weariness. I washed my face in cold water, then opened one of the wheelhouse windows and stuck my head out into the cold night air.

At midnight I made a fresh pot of coffee, and this helped. Barb had told me to call her so she could take the wheel for a couple of hours, but she had looked beaten, and I decided to let her sleep on through. I switched the radio receiver onto the broadcast band and picked up a station playing lively Norwegian songs. I listened until the station went off the air, drank more coffee, checked the bilge—anything to keep busy.

By four o'clock we were halfway between Point Retreat and Rocky Island, the sky was beginning to lighten, and I welcomed it, for the dark part of the night was always the hardest when you were weary. It was like being inside a cocoon, with the steady beat of the engine beneath your feet tending to lull you to sleep.

At four-thirty there was a call on the radiophone. It was the Supreme Commander.

"Wayne, I have the *Lassie* chartered, and Jack Crawley will head out to Taku Inlet immediately. We need you there to do the actual buying . . . could Barbara take the *Apex* on into the cannery, if I send a plane for you?"

I stood there dumbly, until it finally penetrated. *Wasn't there any limit to what Holm would ask of a man?* I wondered.

The Fish Buyers

"Well, what do you think?" the Supreme Commander persisted.

"Stand by," I answered. I stood there a moment thinking. The sea was dead calm; it was perhaps four more hours to the cannery. Barb was not a flighty woman, thank God, and I had shown her how to handle the boat. She knew the way as well as I did. The night's sleep had helped her, so I decided to put it before her and let her make the decision. I adjusted the wheel, then went below to wake her.

She looked out the porthole and saw that it was getting daylight. "Why didn't you call me?" she asked.

"When you get dressed, come up to the wheelhouse," I said.

I went up the ladder to the galley and made another pot of coffee. Presently Barb came up and washed her face at the sink.

"What's up?" she asked as she poured a cup of coffee.

I told her about Holm's request and asked her if she wanted to take the *Apex* on in—or if I should tell Holm no.

"I'll take it in," she said, unconcerned.

I called Holm back and told him.

"Good," he said, "I'll have Ken Loken pick you up. He should be there in forty-five minutes. Where will you be?"

"I'll be off Rocky Island."

"Anything you need?"

"I'll need more money."

"All right, when Ken picks you up, have him fly on to the cannery. You can call them and have the money ready, then Ken will take you back to the *Lassie*, which should be just entering Taku Inlet. Okay?"

"Okay," I said, and signed off.

When I had contacted the cannery, I asked them to have $30,000 cash ready for me and told them Barb would be bringing the *Apex I* in.

Barb cooked breakfast and we ate in turn. I kept thinking of things to tell her: to keep a check on the bilge pumps, to watch the current as she came alongside the fish elevator at the cannery, of this, of that. We finished the coffee, made more, and I kept looking into the northeastern sky for the plane. Presently I saw it with the glasses, a mere dot.

A few minutes later Ken buzzed us, and I cut the throttle and threw the engine out of gear. I put my cash box into a hand bag, along with several books of fish tickets, my toothbrush, a supply of cigars, and I was ready. Ken had landed on the water and was taxiing toward us. I gave Barb last-minute instructions, which I realized were nothing but reassurance for myself, then caught the wing of the plane as it drifted up. Grabbing my bag, I stepped off onto one of the pontoons and climbed in beside Ken. He gunned the engine and the plane went up on the step—then he pulled back on the wheel and we were airborne.

The cannery bookkeeper was waiting at the airplane float for us, and had the money in a canvas bank bag. I took it and got back in. Soon we were in the air again. Ken must have known I was worried about Barb, for he flew back down the shoreline instead of crossing the mountains. A few minutes later we could see the minute *Apex* below: it had gone around Rocky Island and was headed up the shore toward the cannery. Ken dropped down low

The Fish Buyers

and we flew by just above the water. Barb was at the wheel and waved to us.

We began to gain altitude, and Ken looked at me and said, "Quite some wife you've got, Wayne."

"Yes," I said, extremely proud of her.

14

Salmon Run!

It was nearly eight o'clock when we sighted the *Lassie* steaming into the entrance of Taku Inlet. I told Ken to make a swing around the inlet before we landed, for I wanted some idea of how many boats were fishing there, and of how heavily they were loaded down. We passed over the *Lassie* and swept low over the water as I began to check the boats.

Taku Inlet was roughly fifteen miles long from Point Bishop to Taku Point, where the river actually began, and approximately three miles wide at its farthest point. The inlet was alive with gill netters; I counted over 150 of them, then lost track. The nets seemed to cover the entire inlet so thoroughly that one wondered if it were at all possible for a salmon coming home to spawn to elude them and escape into the river itself.

We came in low over Taku Point, circled the impressive Taku Glacier, and came back down the opposite shore. The Indian skiffs off Flat Point were so overloaded

Salmon Run!

with fish that many of them were on the point of capsizing. I realized if I were to service the boats on a first-come-first-serve basis, I would have a full load long before I could work my way up to Flat Point. I asked Ken to land, and after a moment he found a spot free of nets and set the little plane down on the water. We turned, and taxied back to where a long string of Indian skiffs were anchored in a line as they patiently waited for the next tender. Ken shut off the engine, and I opened the door and climbed out onto a pontoon. One of the Indians was a man I knew well, Willie Jim. I called to him, and after giving me a puzzled look, he started his outboard motor and came over to where we drifted with the current.

"What's the situation, Willie?" I asked.

"Lotsa fish, I tell you. Boats all waiting for tender—can't fish—skiffs he sink. Where you come from, by golly?"

I explained to Willie that I had flown back from the cannery and was going aboard the *Lassie*, which was just coming into the inlet now. I told him I could never make it up to Flat Point before being loaded, and that he should pass the word to all the rest of the skiff rigs to come down the inlet to meet me.

"Very good," Willie said, "I do that."

Twenty minutes later I was aboard the *Lassie*, and I waved to Ken as he headed back to Juneau. The *Lassie* was a halibut and black-cod boat, perhaps forty-eight feet in length. It had been laid up in Juneau after the halibut season, and Holm was able to charter it. Jack Crawley, the owner-skipper, turned the wheel over to me, and I told him he had better get a bite to eat before the rush began. He just grinned at me and shook his head. I knew he had a rude awakening coming, for there probably would not be a chance to eat until we were loaded and headed for the cannery. By that time we would be so weary we probably would not care about food. I had caught my second wind, however, and I felt pretty good.

An alert gill netter ahead spotted us. He quickly reeled in his net and came our way at full throttle. Now some of the others saw us. I slowed down the engine and threw it into neutral. As Jack and I took the first gill netter's line, we saw the horde descending upon us.

"Holy cow!" Jack exclaimed.

"You haven't seen anything yet," I said to him.

Then the fish began to come aboard, while the *Lassie* sank little by little into the sea. Jack had brought a set of platform scales from Juneau, and both of us pitched fish into the big steel box which sat on top of the scales. Each boxload weighed around 1,000 pounds, and when it was full, Jack called out the weight to me and I went into the galley and made out the fish ticket. While I was paying the fisherman, Jack dumped the load into the hold and was pitching in the next man's fish from the opposite side. Some of the fishermen had close to $1,000 coming for the two days of fishing, and the few $500 bills I had were extremely popular. One of the men whose lines I chopped loose yesterday was a little stand-offish with me as he pitched his fish aboard, but when he came into the galley to collect his money I gave him a stiff drink of whiskey, and we were friends again.

By midnight we had close to 30,000 pounds of fish aboard, and still they came. I had called Holm and requested another tender, and he promised to have one on the way soon. Many of the boats which sold first had gone

Salmon Run!

back to fishing and now were ready to sell again, and still there were many calling on the radiophone for me to pick up their fish. The night had turned dark with low overcast, and a brisk southeaster brought a chop to the waters of the inlet. This made it hard to see the corks of the gill nets as I maneuvered the heavily loaded *Lassie* between them. The fishermen were required to have lights on the loose ends of the nets, but some of them were out, and it was extremely tricky. If I made a mistake and ran through a gill net it would undoubtedly get wound up in the *Lassie*'s propeller, and if this occurred, we were out of business.

Jack stood beside me at the wheel. "I don't see how you do it," he said.

"It just takes practice." We ran on slowly, stopping to take fish aboard, and still the radiophone was busy as boats called us. They were out in the dark somewhere, and I had to twist and turn my way through the nets to find them. Some of them tried my patience, for had they not been so afraid of losing a little fishing time, they could have unloaded earlier.

Just before dawn we had a brief respite, and Jack cooked a big T-bone steak for each of us. I kicked the *Lassie* out of gear and hurriedly ate for the first time in twenty hours. We washed down the steak and toast with scalding coffee—then the boats were upon us once more with first light. I was rummy now with fatigue; my brain too weary to think. We worked by instinct alone, and there were blank spaces in my mind. For instance, a moment ago, we were still dumping salmon into the hold, and now I saw we had put the hatch covers on and were dumping them into the bait hold. I didn't recall changing over, and I wondered if Jack did. I was still making out fish tickets and paying out large sums of money, and hoped I hadn't made any mistakes.

Soon the bait hold was full; we stamped on the fish in our rubber hip boots to settle them and make room for a few more. At last we were forced to put on the hatch cover and batten it down. There were now several inches of water over the well deck. I got bin boards and nailed them alongside the deckhouse, then we began to pitch the fish upon the foredeck. We were at the point of having to refuse any more fish and leave, when I looked up and saw a big limit seiner coming.

It was the *Yukon Maid,* and Harry, the Thlinget skipper, came within hailing distance and told me he was to replace the *Lassie.*

I called to the gill netters alongside and told them the *Lassie* was going to the cannery, and I would move aboard the *Yukon Maid* and resume buying. They untied and Harry brought the *Yukon Maid* alongside for me. I gathered up the fish-ticket books, the cash box, and my cigars. Jack and I shook hands, then I picked up my things and stepped out on deck. Already boats were tied on the *Yukon Maid*'s off side. I climbed wearily onto the seiner and deposited my gear on the galley table. We let loose Jack's lines, and he moved sluggishly down the inlet, the seas running in and out of the scuppers.

Harry had brought another man with him, and for this I was thankful. I let the two of them do the fish pitching and weighing up, and as they called out the weights I made out the tickets and paid off the fishermen. This speeded up the operation considerably. Harry said the *Yukon Maid* would carry something over 70,000 pounds,

Salmon Run!

and I hoped we would be able to service all the boats in Taku Inlet.

We worked on through the night, and by first light the following morning we were loaded, and headed up Stephen's Passage for the cannery. I rolled fully dressed into a bunk, and quietly died for five hours.

Harry awoke me. I sat up and rubbed the sleep from my eyes; the wall clock said ten o'clock. "Where are we?" I asked.

"Off Point Retreat," he said. "You wife bring the *Apex I* from cannery."

"Where?" I asked, and pulled on my boots.

"She coming up to us now."

I stepped into the wheelhouse and looked out; the *Apex* was steaming straight for us, perhaps a mile away. Harry slowed down and kicked the clutch out of gear. I went back into the galley and washed up, then poured coffee. Harry explained that the cannery was swamped with fish and several of the other tenders were lying at the fish elevator waiting to be unloaded. The only available tender was the *Apex*, and Holm had talked Barb into bringing it out to meet us. I was to go aboard and return to the fishing grounds.

Presently the *Apex* was within a hundred yards of us. Barb slowed down and drifted while Harry moved alongside. I gathered my things, said good-by to Harry, and stepped aboard.

Jim Brown had returned from Portland Canal to take over Taku Inlet, and we went back to Port Snettisham. During this three-day period I had loaded five tenders, for a total of 210,000 pounds of fish.

The next three weeks were one continuous nightmare. Never once did the spawning salmon let up until the season closed on the twentieth of September. The notorious equinoctial storms had begun, and on our last trip to the cannery with the *Apex I* dangerously overloaded, we took a vicious beating between Point Retreat and the cannery. Southeasterly winds of sixty knots and more produced mountainous seas which pounded the ancient vessel hour upon hour, until the caulking loosened and the hull began to leak like a sieve. Finally, after sixteen frightening hours we limped into the cannery with two power-driven pumps working steadily, and Barb at the wheel while I operated the hand deck pump. We were utterly beaten.

While the *Apex I* was being unloaded I had Holm call a plane out from Juneau to fly Barb and Mark home to Warm Springs Bay. Barb was several months pregnant, and now, after the terrifying trip in on the badly leaking *Apex I*, I realized what a fool I had been to subject Mark and her to such danger.

Ken Loken flew in that afternoon to pick them up. After promising Barb I wouldn't take the *Apex I* out again, I said good-by to Mark and her, and watched the departing plane until it disappeared in the southern sky.

The following day I flew to Juneau to take over *Lassie*. The Supreme Commander had chartered the boat to help out the *Neptune* at Chilkat Inlet, and I brought her back to the cannery to wait out the decision on a proposed extension of the season in Lynn Canal.

A few hours later the extension was confirmed by the Fish and Wildlife Service, and I filled the fuel tanks and got groceries aboard.

15

A Night to Remember

"Here's the deal," Holm said. "I've promised Elton Engstrom, in Juneau, a load of bright dog salmon for the fresh-fish market. I want you to take *Lassie* up to Chilkat Inlet, and if the dogs look pretty bright, buy a load and run them into town. If they're too badly colored, then bring them back here for canning. Okay?"

"What about a deck hand?"

"How about getting one of the local Indians to go with you? I think Paul Billy would be just the fellow; he's a good boatman."

"Drink?"

"Never touches it," Holm said.

Sunday evening I walked down toward the village. I did not feel well at all, and I thought I was coming down with the flu. But when you are a tender skipper running a non-union boat and there is no one to take your place —you keep going until you drop.

The village was the usual haphazard arrangement

of rundown shacks. These company villages all look and smell alike to a white man, but apparently they do not offend the occupants in the least. This one reeked of half-rotten fish, or outdoor privies and decaying garbage. I saw children playing and heard their laughter in the clear evening air; there was the sound of rock and roll music on a nearby radio, and in the background was the soft lisping Thlinget tongue as oldsters gossiped on their front steps.

After much questioning I learned that Paul Billy lived on the far edge of the village, and there was a small totem with a raven on top in his front yard.

There was no harmony in the Billy household today, for Mrs. Billy answered the door with a black eye and two front teeth missing. She was under the impression I was the "jail man" who had come to take her drunken, crazed husband away. She readily told me he was hiding under the house, and offered to help me capture him in any way she could. I went around to the back and peered warily into the dark cavern beneath the house, but I could not see him. "Hey, Paul!" I yelled. "You want job? Make big money; see the world through porthole, huh?"

"Sombitch, you! Go 'way!" A rock thudded against the post by my head, and I hastily retreated.

To hell with it, anyway, I thought. *I'll go and tell the Supreme Commander a thing or two!* I headed back toward the company office.

I found out that Holm had flown off to Ketchikan, so at last I went down to the *Hannah C,* where Duke and Dutch and all the rest of the tender men were gathered around a bottle. I helped myself to a drink and we dis-

A Night to Remember

cussed ways of getting Paul Billy from beneath his domicile without being cut up or hit in the head with a rock.

"There's only one thing that'll bring him out from under the house," Jim Brown said with authority, "and that's whiskey."

"He might be drunk, but he's sly as a fox," I said. "If you go up there and offer him a drink, you won't get anything but a rock for your trouble."

"I think Jim's right about the whiskey," Duke said. "We'll take up a bottle with a little firewater in it and put it out in the open on the ground. Then we'll all hide, and when he comes out to get it, all of us will pile onto him and tie him up."

So our decision made, we took part of a bottle of whiskey, some nine-thread buoy line, and the whole bunch of us went back to the village. Mrs. Billy said her husband was still under the house and we called to him and placed the bottle in the middle of the foot path.

"Come on out, Paul," we called solicitously. "Have a drink with your friends."

No answer.

"You hurt us, Paul, when you act this way!" Duke cried. "Come out, old friend, and we'll drink to the Raven Clan."

No answer.

We passed the bottle around, loudly smacking our lips over the quality of the whiskey. When this didn't work, we set the whiskey bottle in the center of the foot path and eased away. Presently all was quiet. Many of the village people had gathered down the roadway in the fading light and were watching us curiously, wondering what the crazy white men could be up to now. We sat quietly on our haunches and waited in the shadows, our eyes focused on the bottle of whiskey.

All at once, after ten silent minutes, Paul Billy streaked through the gap in the boards beneath the house and lunged for the bottle. At the same instant all of us piled onto him and held the wild Indian down. Dutch had been delegated to hog-tie him, and he began to get his lines ready, but he became confused with all the squirming bodies and flailing limbs and ended up tying Duke's leg to one of Bob Horchover's. When at last this error was discovered, all of us began to untangle ourselves, and in the confusion, Paul Billy got loose and would have surely gotten away—and with our whiskey—had it not been for Mrs. Billy, who had stood by with a pue handle waiting for a chance to get even. She hit her spouse a good one behind the ear, and it was all over.

We tied up Paul Billy, borrowed a coal cart, and transported him back to the docks, where he was dumped into the *Lassie*'s fo'c'sle to sober up. The rest of the posse went back to the *Hannah C* to open another bottle, and presently Duke and I could hear them bragging about how efficiently we had captured Billy.

I made a pot of coffee and Duke and I sat at the galley table sipping it. "Well, only a few more days and it'll be all over," Duke said. "Then we can go home."

"I'm ready," I said, and the two of us sat silent with our thoughts.

At one o'clock that night I got up by the alarm and put on the coffeepot. I started the diesel engine and surveyed friend Billy who was sleeping, still tied up on the fo'c'sle floor. When the engine temperature was up to

A Night to Remember

normal, I untied the lines and carried a cup of coffee into the wheelhouse; I backed the *Lassie* into the channel and headed out the bay.

I stood before the wheel with a peculiar feeling in my stomach. For the past few days I had felt pretty rough, but I had thought it was because I had been so tired. Now I knew it was the flu, for my joints ached and I was sweating and had diarrhea. As time went on it was pure misery to stay at the wheel. The *Lassie* was equipped with an automatic pilot, but it was out of order, so I kept checking on Paul Billy to see if he had come alive.

Finally, as we were coming up on Danger Point, I looked into the fo'c'sle and saw that Paul was awake. I left the wheel and went below. His eyes studied me curiously, and he seemed to be among the sane. "How do you feel, Paul?" I asked.

"Not so good—my head, goddam, he hurt like hell!"

"That's because your wife clobbered you with a pue handle," I said, and untied him. I gave him a change of clothing. "Go up on deck and wash up; the fresh air will help you."

Twenty minutes later he came into the wheelhouse and stood in silence as he leaned against the open window. After a while he spoke: "What I do this tam?"

"You closed one of your wife's eyes and knocked out two of her front teeth; I guess you were pretty rough with your kids before you got run out of the house."

The faint light from the compass touched his dark features, and I saw a look of anguish there. He stared out into the darkness for a long time. Finally he asked, "You ever see Indian whip childs?"

"No," I said honestly, "I don't believe I ever did."

"Indian believe when baby born, he spirit of somebody in family that die long tam ago—you no hit old-tam peoples, huh? That's why you no whip childs."

I lit a cigar and pondered the thing I'd just heard. For years I had wondered why the Indian children were left to do pretty much as they pleased; now, in the night, a man tormented because he had struck his children had explained it all.

Paul Billy might have been a wife beater and child beater when drunk, but he was a boatman all the way through. As we ran in the dark night, he had no way of knowing where we were headed, but one glance at the compass was enough. "What for we go to Haines?" he asked.

"We're going up to Chilkat Inlet to buy a load of dog salmon, then run them into Juneau."

"I working for you?"

"That's right, Paul—I'll pay you one hundred and fifty dollars for the trip."

He brightened visibly. "I gonna buy old woman and childs some presents in Juneau."

"Fine. You in shape to take the wheel for a while?"

"Good shape," Paul said, and I turned the wheel over to him and went back into the galley. I rolled up my coat for a pillow and stretched out on the bench. Once or twice I stepped out on deck to see how Paul was doing; then, satisfied, I lay down and drifted off into a feverish sleep that was filled with distorted dreams of the *Lassie* sinking from an overload of fish. The gill netters came on endlessly, pitching fish aboard until at last the boat slipped beneath the sea....

A bitter northerly wind was blowing as we passed

A Night to Remember

Sullivan Island and began to enter Chilkat Inlet, and presently it started to snow.

"October bad tam in dis country," Paul said, and I was ready to believe it. We ran up into a small cove on the right-hand side of the bottleneck and dropped the anchor. Many of the gill netters had seen us pass, and we knew they would start coming pretty soon.

"How 'bout breakfast while we have chance?" Paul asked, and though I had no appetite, I knew I must eat to get through the day. I nodded, and Paul washed up at the sink, and presently he had ham and eggs on the table.

All that day we bought fish, and the *Lassie* slowly sank into the sea. The dog salmon were bright, which indicated a new school had moved in recently; they tend to turn various shades of red, yellow, green and black if they are long exposed to the fresh water from the rivers. I decided to take them to Engstrom in Juneau when we had a load.

The flu had me weak as a kitten, and I was as sick as I had ever been in my life. After a frantic race to the toilet on the far side of the deckhouse, I would creep back with every last vestige of strength gone, and fill out fish slips as Paul Billy weighed up the fish and called out their weights.

At midnight we had a load. I talked to Duke on the *Hannah C;* he had been dispatched at the last minute to relieve us. They were taking a beating around Rocky Island, he said, adding that he and Dutch had also come down with the flu during the night.

Paul Billy and I pulled the anchor and I headed the *Lassie* south. The wind was savage, coming in gusts from fifty to sixty miles per hour, and Paul and I both knew we had a chore ahead of us this night, for Eldred Rock had earlier reported a nine-foot sea. Before we got out into the strait itself, I had Paul spike down the bail hold hatch and tighten the turnbuckles on the chains that secured the lifeboat on the stern. While he did this, I went below to the engine room and drained the water trap on the fuel lines, just in case. We were as ready now as we'd ever be; I cracked open the throttle and we quartered into it, the heavily laden *Lassie* rolling abominably.

Paul, good boatman that he was, stowed everything movable away, and we continued to quarter before the sea until we had reached the center of Lynn Canal. I turned *Lassie's* stern right into it then, and the work began. The mammoth seas rolled up from behind, completely covering the aft deck, and smashed against the back of the deckhouse. *Lassie* would heel and shear off, and it took real skill at the wheel to keep her from broaching. The sea would pour out of the scuppers as she rose sluggishly up out of the trough, then another big one would roll over the sunken stern again. I turned the wheel over to Paul, and after a few minutes realized that he knew his business. I left him and walked back to the galley door and switched on the afterdeck light, then watched in fascination as a big whitecapped wave rolled up from behind, towered a split second over the stern, then crashed down upon us until the whole afterdeck disappeared in the sea. It was frightening. Slowly *Lassie* would raise and shed the sea and ready herself for the next onslaught. In times like these, a man is as close to a vessel as he can possibly be. The engine pounding away steadily below is like a human heartbeat, and sometimes it seems in tune with your own. You are so utterly de-

A Night to Remember

pendent upon it that a vessel takes on the aspects of a personal friend, and it is not hard to understand why some owners refuse to part with an old and rotten and outdated vessel.

I turn off the afterdeck light and move back into the wheelhouse. As I brace myself against the roll, I see Paul Billy's dark features in the dim glow from the compass light, and there is the quality of an eagle about his high cheekbones and aquiline nose. He is an entirely different man than the one who twenty-four hours ago lay drunken on the fo'c'sle floor.

On this stormy night, however, with violent death only a hairbreadth away, Paul Billy and I are as close as two men can be. The wind and sea become worse, and we keep slowing down until we barely have steerage. Each time the diesel engine misses a beat we hold our breath, for if it were to fail us now, or the tiller chain should break—we are lost. . . .

16

End of the Season

The distance from Chilkat Inlet to Juneau is roughly ninety miles, and it took Paul Billy and me twenty-two miserable hours to make it—about twice the normal running time. When at last we pulled into the Juneau cold storage dock, I was completely beaten. After our lines were secured, I left Paul to oversee the unloading and I staggered uptown and took a room at the Gastineau Hotel, where I immediately undressed and got into bed.

The following morning I shaved and bathed and changed into clean clothing, then forced myself across the street to see Doc Carter. It was the Asian flu, and I had a temperature of 103 degrees. Doc was all ready to send me to the hospital, but I've always thought of hospitals as only the last resort, so I talked him into giving me some penicillin pills, then went back to my room fortified with a bottle of spirits. I fixed myself a good hot toddy, then got back into that wonderful bed.

About ten the next morning there was a knock on the door, and when I opened it there stood Paul Billy. I asked

End of the Season

him in, and he reported he had seen to the unloading of the fish, scrubbed down the fish hold, then moved the *Lassie* over to the boat harbor. He wanted to know if there was anything else I wanted done.

I told him there wasn't, and got out my cash box and opened it. "Paul," I said, "this is the last trip, and since Juneau is the *Lassie*'s home port we'll leave her tied right where she is. Now, then, you have one hundred and fifty dollars coming, and I'll also pay your plane fare home. Why don't you take this morning's flight out?"

Paul looked down at the floor, and I well knew what was in his mind. Finally he said, "I like to stay in town two, tree day—visit old fren'."

I knew that Paul's "old fren' " came out of a bottle and was his worst enemy. I really hated to see him get started again, but I couldn't change him, so I said, "All right, but how about me giving you fifty dollars, and sending the rest home to your wife?"

Paul kept looking at the floor, but said nothing.

"Paul, fifty bucks, if properly spent, will give you all the hangover you could possibly want."

He grinned sheepishly. "I want buy old woman and childs present, too."

"Then let's give you seventy-five, and send the rest of it home, okay?"

I could clearly see that Paul wanted the whole $150, but at last he agreed to my terms, and I paid him. He carefully folded the bills and put them in his trouser pocket. I held out my hand and we shook. "Paul," I said, "you're a good boatman and it was a pleasure having you."

"I like work with you," he said. "You need me sometam more, you call on Paul Billy, huh?"

Paul turned then and went out into the hallway and down the stairs. The next morning he was arrested for being drunk and disorderly, and began a five-day sentence in jail.

That afternoon I crept out of bed and began to total up the number of pounds of salmon I had bought during the past three months since Barb and Mark and I had moved aboard *Apex I*. The total came to a little less than one million pounds, and at the one-cent-a-pound commission Holm and I had agreed upon I had almost ten thousand dollars coming. This was pretty good money in one light, but thinking back to all we had been through —I figured we had earned every bit of it.

I dressed and went down the street to the bank to settle my affairs. Deducting my commission, I drew a bank draft in the Supreme Commander's name for the balance of my buying fund. At the same time I made out a money order to Mrs. Billy, put it in an envelope addressed to her, and dropped it into the mailbox on the way out.

Stopping by the Alaska Coastal Airlines office on the waterfront, I purchased a ticket in Paul Billy's name, informing them that Paul would undoubtedly try to cash in the ticket as soon as he was released from jail. I asked them to shove him into a plane and send him home when he did so.

As I walked along the Alaska Steamship dock to check in with Elton Engstrom, I saw the *Hannah C* coming up Gastineau Channel, heavily loaded. I stood there in front of Engstrom's office watching them ease in toward the unloading dock. Presently Engstrom came

End of the Season

down the stairs from his office, a big florid man in his fifties.

"You look like hell, Wayne," he said, sticking out a hand.

"I feel like it, too."

"Looks like your brothers took a beating," he said, pointing to the *Hannah C.* "They had ninety-mile-an-hour winds and fourteen-foot seas in Lynn Canal last night."

I shivered, just thinking about it.

The *Hannah C* was alongside the dock now, and Engstrom and I climbed down the ladder and helped Dutch get lines around the dock piling. Presently we had the boat secured, the hatch directly below the electric unloading hoist.

Duke climbed down the ladder from the bridge. He was bearded and dirty, eyes red and watering from fatigue. "What a trip," he said at last. "Lost the lifeboat and one of the galley doors; the chains holding the range down parted and it got loose and tore everything in the galley all to hell! Nothing to eat since we left Chilkat . . . no coffee . . . a hellish sea washing plumb across the waist . . ."

Engstrom shook his head. "Glad I'm just a fish buyer," he said. "How much fish you got, Duke?"

"A hundred and six thousand pounds."

"You boys take off," Engstrom said, "I'll get a crew down and have them start unloading . . . probably take us all night."

"Where are you staying?" Duke asked me.

"At the Gastineau."

"Okay," he said to Engstrom, "give us a call when you

got the old girl unloaded and Dutch and I will come down and move her over to the float."

He and Dutch filled a bag with changes of clothing, and we caught a cab back to the hotel. Two hours later the three of us sat in Mike's Place, drinking highballs and waiting for steak dinners. It felt good to sit inside, safe from the sea and wind, knowing the last trip was behind us and we could now go home to our families.

The Supreme Commander flew in from the cannery the following day, and we settled our accounts with him. Duke agreed to return in the spring and skipper a tender for him, but Dutch and I decided we would go back fishing. We shook hands then, and said good-by.

On the flight home we shared the Grumman Goose with Wesley Walker and his Thlinget wife, Sadie. Walker, an industrious man in his middle fifties, had made a great deal of money dismantling salmon canneries. His last job had been the mammoth Libby, McNeil and Libby cannery in Taku Harbor, which he had worked on for the past four years. Now he informed us he had recently purchased the cannery and cold-storage buildings in Murder Cove from Whiz Fish Company, and he and his wife were moving out there to begin dismantling the installation.

As the plane flew south over Admiralty Island I thought of Barb and the baby she would soon have. I had a feeling it would be another boy. You needed sons in this raw land, where it took muscles and sweat and determination to realize your dreams.

Two months later Mike, like Mark, came prematurely. But this time I had insisted that Barb go to town early.

After Barb's return I could see that we would soon

End of the Season

need a larger home, so when Wesley Walker in Murder Cove contacted me two years later and asked if I would like to finish dismantling the salmon cannery there, we began packing once more, for here was an excellent chance to acquire all the materials we would need for the large house we wanted to build.

PART FOUR

17

Murder Cove

Before the arrival of the white man, the Alaskan aboriginals had for countless years depended for survival upon the returning hordes of Pacific salmon. It is unlikely that these people understood the anadromous cycle of salmon at all. They referred to them as the Salmon People, believing that they were a race of supernatural beings who went about in human form dancing and feasting beneath the sea. Then, when it came time for the runs, they assumed the form of fish and ascended the streams to sacrifice themselves for the good of mankind. Consequently, the aboriginals' whole way of life was inextricably tied to the returning salmon, which formed the basis of their totemic culture.

The Thlingets of southeastern Alaska were divided into fourteen loosely confederated territorial tribes, and each of these was subdivided into a number of autonomous local clans which were actually groups of relatives who traced lineage to a common ancestor. Each clan retained possession of its lands and resources; fishing rights were inherited by descendants of the individuals or passed on to the group, and these rights were inviolable. There was no waste, for they harvested only what they needed to live on. Moreover, if a certain stream was barren during the salmon runs, the clan had only to ask permission of one of their more fortunate neighboring clans and, for a tribute in the form of salmon, could fish their waters. Thus a fine balance between the salmon resources and the aboriginal population was maintained.

For hundreds of years this balance was upheld. Then came the Europeans. In 1785 Grigorii Shelikov put up dried salmon for the workers of his fur-trading post on the Karluk River on Kodiak Island. There was a world of salmon, but outside of salting or drying enough for winter use, what good were they commercially?

In the early 1800's a few salmon were salted and taken to the States, but these ventures did not succeed. It was not until 1864 that the Hume Brothers of California were able to put salmon in cans and process them successfully. Within a few years salmon canneries were located all along the coast from California to Puget Sound. In 1878, eleven years after the United States purchased Alaska from Russia, the first two salmon canneries were established in Alaska. The rush was now on to establish other canneries all over the Territory—and a new era began to emerge. It was an industry that had far surpassed the fur era, and would surpass the gold rush.

Yet none of these early-day cannery men gave a thought to conservation; there seemed to be an endless supply of salmon, and they used every method imaginable to catch the returning fish. The fish traps, however, were

Murder Cove

the cheapest and most effective manner of catching the salmon, and they were used for the next eighty years—until at last, with statehood, the traps were finally abolished. But by that time it was too late. What a few conservationists had been preaching for the past fifty years had fallen on the deaf ears of the absentee owners of the big packing companies (less than ten percent of the companies were owned by Alaskans). This ruthless exploitation by companies controlled by New York and San Francisco and Seattle finally began to tell. The U.S. Fish and Wildlife Service, instead of controlling the salmon industry, had in effect been controlled by it. In a twenty-year period—from 1940 until statehood in 1959—the annual salmon pack dropped from 7,000,000 cases to 1,500,000.

Consequently, many of the canneries that dotted the bays of southeastern Alaska began to close down. Some of the smaller ones were bankrupt; many of the larger companies survived by suspending operations in some of their plants and merging with other companies in an effort to cut costs. The new order of the day became merger, consolidation and custom canning. Few of the canneries that had been shut down ever processed another fish. Almost without exception they were finally sold and dismantled; the lumber, various materials and machinery were sold piecemeal.

With statehood, the newly created Department of Fish and Game imposed strict regulations upon fishing boats and gear alike. They hired scores of marine biologists to study the problems, and began to think seriously of hatcheries, pointing out the gains Oregon, Washington and British Columbia had made in this direction. But it

— THIS RAW LAND —

would take them many years to undo the work of the avaricious cannery men who had held the industry in their tenacious grip for so many years.

Now Barb and I and our sons were moving to Murder Cove to finish wrecking the cannery. Walker had spent the previous two years at this task; but he had contracted to begin dismantling still another cannery in Peril Strait and had asked me if I was interested in spending the winter in Murder Cove and finish up the job. He offered to split fifty-fifty everything I was able to salvage. He had a ready market for all materials, and I was free to keep whatever I wished for my personal use. I had looked over the remains of the cannery and saw that much of the lumber was of a quality you could not buy these days, and I would be able to get almost everything I would need for the large house Barb and I wanted to build.

I had agreed to work there throughout the winter until the fishing season began in the spring. This was acceptable to Walker, so on a day in early September we loaded our things aboard the *Wooden Shoe*, got the boys and our dog, Fink, aboard, and headed for Murder Cove.

It was late evening when we pulled into the harbor and tied up at the float. As we unloaded, it began to rain. I found a large four-wheel fish cart on the dock and Barb and I began to load it. The boys were running up and down the dock yelling, and Fink, our red spaniel, was barking excitedly behind them. Barb and I wheeled the cart up the boardwalk between the deserted cannery buildings to the former superintendent's cottage, where Walker and his wife had stayed. We moved everything inside, and I started the oil stove for Barb.

Murder Cove

As Mark and I went back for another load, the wind howled between the empty buildings, banging loose doors and rattling windows. The rain, slanting ahead of the wind, soon soaked us through to our skins, and while we carried boxes up the ramp and stacked them onto the cart, doubts about bringing my family to this isolated spot began to assail me. We were miles from another living soul, separated by the awesome mountains and the unpredictable sea. Ahead of us lay the savage winter storms. We had no electricity, no running water; stove oil and groceries would have to be freighted in from Juneau on the mailboat, *Yakobi,* which made weekly stops if the weather permitted. I was used to this sort of life, but I worried about Barb and the boys. What if one of them became sick, or was badly hurt?

When Mark and I returned with our load, the stove had warmed the kitchen and Barb had a pot of coffee ready.

"You found the well?"

Barb nodded. "It's over by the old cookhouse. How did they get water here when the cannery ran?"

"They had four-inch wood-stave pipe running clear to the head of the bay, and pumped water three miles down here to those big redwood tanks you see out by the old powerhouse."

"Mike and I went to the garden and found some raspberries and strawberries—and you know what?"

"What?"

"A beautiful doe and her last spring's fawn stood there in the rain and watched us for the longest time."

"Lots of deer here, all right—bears, too," I said. "We'll have to keep a sharp eye on the boys."

It was getting dark now, and I dug out the Aladdin lamp and lit it. As I changed into dry clothing, Barb began fixing supper, humming a little tune to herself. Most women would have thrown up their hands in despair if you moved them into such a place. My earlier fears were quickly dispelled. Everything was going to work out fine.

Walker warned me of the brown bear he had seen around the cannery last summer, and we were well settled before we began to have trouble with them. One evening Mark and I walked back onto a large muskeg not far behind the cannery and sat down with my rifle to blow a deer call. On the third call a doe came running out of the forest into the open. A moment later two bucks followed her. I shot the larger buck in the head, then the other one through the ribs as he turned to run back toward the woods.

I dressed both and made them up into packs, leaving one beneath a tree at the edge of the muskeg. I squirmed into the shoulder straps of the other and got to my feet with the buck on my back.

An hour later we were back to pick up the buck we had left. It was dusk now, and as we crossed the muskeg toward the tree where I had stashed the buck, I spotted a bear standing over the deer carcass.

I stopped, slipping the rifle sling from my shoulder. "Bear, Marky!" I said, sliding a cartridge into the chamber.

"Where?" Mark asked.

I squatted down on my heels, pointing until my small son saw the motionless bear beneath the tree.

"Are you gonna shoot him, Dad?"

I didn't know the answer to his question. We had

enough distance between us so that we weren't in too much danger. I could take a rest on a mossy hummock and very likely put the bear down with one shot. Ten years before, I would have killed the animal without a moment's hesitation. But somehow I'd changed since then, I realized suddenly.

"We've got a deer home," I said finally. "Should we let the brownie have this one to eat, Marky?"

"Maybe he's real hungry."

"Yes, perhaps he is." I stood up, speaking softly to Mark: "Turn around and start back the way we came slowly—I'll be right behind you."

Five minutes later we were on the far edge of the muskeg and into the woods.

It was dusk when we came out of the woods and onto the sandy beach of Murder Cove. We sat down on a log and I took the cartridge from the chamber of my rifle, then lit a cigar. The cry of geese came faintly from the north. A little later their cries were louder; then we saw the big V of Canadian honkers gliding in over the treetops as they came in to land in the grass flats of the cove.

"Why didn't we shoot him?" Mark asked abruptly. He had broken off a blueberry branch in the woods, and now picked the berries off one by one and popped them into his mouth. I knew he was thinking about all the stories he had heard my brothers and me tell of the bears we'd killed in the past. I suddenly wished I had the answers. I knew that at thirty-three years old I had a much different outlook than I had at twenty-three. How would I be thinking at forty-three? But I had to find an answer for my son.

— THIS RAW LAND —

"We have to kill deer to eat, don't we?" He nodded. "But we can't eat brownies—too strong and tough, huh?" Mark agreed by shaking his head, his blue eyes looking solemnly at me. "So we don't want to kill an animal we can't possibly use, do we?"

"But what if a bear tries to eat *us*?"

"Then we'll have to shoot him," I said, taking his hand, and we walked along the beach toward the house.

It was a bad year for the brown bear, for the usual run of spawning salmon which they largely depended upon to lay on fat for winter hibernation had not come. As a rule, during this time of year, the brownies would be concentrated along the large salmon streams that emptied into the head of the bay. Now, in desperation, they began to patrol the beaches as they searched for anything edible. One afternoon I counted six bear on the beach across the bay.

The next morning I stepped out of the house to find a huge pile of bear manure twenty feet from the front door. It was still warm. I returned to the house and warned Barb and the boys, then stepped outside with my .30–06, Fink ahead, nose to the trail. I slid a cartridge into the chamber and went around the side of the house, following the path of the bear through the knee-high grass. It led unerringly to our meat house, an ancient building with hand-hewn yellow-cedar studding, which had been a bunkhouse back in the days when Tyee had been a whaling station. The door and windows were gone, but I hung our venison and fish high off the floor so smaller animals such as weasels and mink, or a stray land otter couldn't reach it.

Of the deer Mark and I had brought in a few days

before, there remained only a torn piece of one front quarter. I went out through the open doorway on the far side of the building, picking up the trail in the high grass. It veered down onto the beach and crossed the soft earth of the tide flats, where a good set of prints told me it was a bear weighing perhaps five hundred pounds. I followed the prints above the high-tide line, then lost them as they cut back into the forest's bed of spruce needles.

Back at the house I laid down a strict set of rules for Mark and Mike: they were to confine their play area to the front porch until I could kill the meat thief. I spent the rest of the day watching the beaches. I saw bear across the bay, but our friend did not show; he was no doubt holed up gorging off the deer carcass he'd carried away.

My luck was no better that night; I had nailed boards over the rear exit of the meat house, then hung the mangled front quarter up high for bait. Rigging a flashlight on the back part of the house, I sat there in the dark with my rifle until one o'clock in the morning, but the bear did not show. Finally, stiff and cold, I gave up and went to bed.

At seven the following morning, Mark came running into our bedroom and poked me. "Dad!" he cried, "the bear is coming out of the meat house!" I jumped out of bed, ran into the front room and lifted the .30–06 from the gun rack. Jacking a shell into the chamber, I flipped on the safety, and went into the kitchen where Mark and Mike had their noses pressed against the windowpanes.

"See him, Dad!" Mark yelled.

"Bear," Mike said solemnly, pointing a forefinger.

There he was, sure enough, a big dark-brown brute lumbering unconcerned down the beach and across the tide flats where Fink and I had followed his tracks yesterday. I slid the kitchen window open, laying the rifle across the sill. He was broadside now, the distance perhaps 150 yards. I put the gold bead of the sight on his shoulder and squeezed the trigger.

Off he went with a tremendous burst of speed, then he was down. I put another bullet into the massive head, and he lay still.

Barb, a sound sleeper, had not awakened when Mark came into the bedroom to wake me. Now, with deafening sounds of the shots making our ears ring, she came running into the kitchen in her nightgown, a terrified look on her face.

"Dad killed the bear! Dad killed the bear!" Mark yelled, jumping up and down.

"Bear," little Mike said solemnly, pointing.

It was too much for Barb: the deafening shots, Fink howling to be let out, and Mark yelling and jumping up and down. "What—" she began, then stopped.

"Start some coffee," I said, "and then we'll tell you all about it."

As I went back to the bedroom I could hear Mark explaining. He and Mike had been up early playing, when Mark looked out of their bedroom window and saw the brownie coming out of the meat house.

When we were dressed, I picked up the rifle, reloaded, and with the two boys following, went down to the beach to where the bear lay, Fink running ahead yipping excitedly.

The bear had the thick, dark-brown hair of the

Murder Cove

Shiras brown bear, which is found only on Admiralty Island, and I decided to skin the animal and smoke-tan the hide for the floor of the boys' bedroom. . . .

Like the buffalo, the grizzly was very nearly exterminated during the first fifty years of the settlement of the West. Once these awesome creatures ranged from northern Mexico, east as far as Minnesota, and northward into Canada and Alaska. Since one of Sutter's men first discovered the coveted yellow metal on the banks of the Sacramento River in 1848 and the hordes of gold seekers headed west, the great golden bear were systematically hunted down and killed. Today, there are possibly less than 1,500 grizzlies left in the western United States, including those in national parks and game reserves. The last stronghold of the grizzly is in remote areas of western Canada, and in Alaska. Very likely Admiralty Island in southeastern Alaska has the heaviest concentration of grizzlies. It is estimated there are about 1,600 grizzlies and brown bear on Admiralty Island alone— or one per square mile!

Most of us who live in the area simply refer to them as "brownies," although the gentlemen with horn-rimmed spectacles who caliper their skulls and categorize them claim four species of grizzly, as well as the famed Shiras brown bear. The true Shiras brown bear is extremely dark brown. It does not have the blue-black sheen of the true black bear, but at a distance some will appear black.

These bear are not gregarious at best; they are notorious cannibals, in fact. But there appears to be no color segregation problem in their society, and this interbreeding has produced any number of color variations from light brown to almost black. It has also produced different characteristics of the skull that often lead the naturalists to believe they have discovered another species of grizzly or brown bear.

No one knows how the brown bear got on the islands. Deer, who normally live out their lives within a five-mile radius of their birthplace, will on occasion swim fantastic distances between islands. Several times I have been fishing in the middle of the strait and observed deer swimming doggedly from one island to another. Once I spotted a buck in Chatham Strait crossing at a spot where the distance between the two islands was eight miles. I spent the rest of the afternoon following him, until finally he reached the shore, staggered up on the beach and collapsed. An hour later he got shakily to his feet and went off into the woods. What prompts such voyages is a mystery. We know that on islands such as Kupreanof and Kuiu, deer make long swims to escape the wolf packs, but there are no wolves on either Baranof or Admiralty.

Bear, with the exception of the polar species, do not swim such distances. One theory of their island locations is that thousands of years ago, with the end of the Ice Age, the rising ocean flooded the valleys (now our deep-water straits and sounds), isolating the bear on certain islands. If there were black or brown bear on the same island, the blacks were annihilated by their larger cousins, for nowhere on the islands do we find the two living together. The islands of Chichagof, Baranof and Admiralty have brown bear, grizzlies and deer, but no black bear or wolves. On Kuiu and Kupreanof islands there are deer, black bear and wolves.

In *The Cheechakoes,* I told of some of the hair-

Murder Cove

raising experiences my parents, brothers and I had with brownies when we settled in Surprise Harbor fourteen years before. Now it appeared we were in for the same thing here in Murder Cove.

A few days after killing the venison thief, another bear appeared. I had brought in another buck and had him hanging in the meat house. I nailed boards over the rear entrance, and fitted a door on the font and latched it. We usually let Fink sleep inside at night, but now I fixed a bed for him on the back porch, directly across from the meat house, and put him out that night. He eyed me reproachfully, as if to say: "What did I do now?"

Around midnight Fink's hysterical barking brought me bolt upright in bed. I jumped up and ran into the kitchen, where I had left my rifle and flashlight on the table. Jacking a shell into the chamber, I stepped barefoot onto the porch and switched on the flashlight.

A brownie was standing with his back to the meathouse door, looking into the light. Fink stood at the bottom of the steps and barked wildly. I raised my rifle to shoot but couldn't see my sights, because it is almost impossible to hold a light and shoot at the same time. In the meantime the brownie broke and ran. Fink, brave now that the bear was taking off, ran out into the dark after him. At the edge of the woods he stopped, though, barking with confidence, letting the brownie know that if he dared come back, Fink would personally tear him apart. From then on Fink accepted the responsibility of guarding deer meat.

During the following week the brownie, which was a bit smaller than the one I had killed, made trips back to the meat house, but I never saw him. He would come at night, and as soon as Fink began barking he would take off. Sometimes I would find his tracks where he had circled the house. The smell of the deer must have made his mouth water, and I knew he would keep hanging around trying to get at it. All during this time we had to keep the boys inside, for we never knew when he might wander into the yard.

One day the *Repeat* steamed into the bay with our friends Jess and Lucille Padon from Fort Alexander. They were out on a hunting and fishing trip, and we were delighted to see them. After supper that night, they decided to stay a week or so. Jess had a dozen big king salmon iced down in the *Repeat*'s hold, and he said if I'd help him we'd smoke and can them.

Jess was my age, a brute of a man with an impressive full-length beard; he stood six foot three and weighed 250 pounds. Jess had been a cowboy in New Mexico, a mate on a tugboat in the Bering Sea, and a professional wrestler before turning to commercial fishing. His wife, Lou, was a slim, dark-haired woman with a very pleasant manner. She and Barb had a fine time visiting.

Jess had told me some of his experiences as a wrestler, where they would put on exhibitions wrestling black bear and alligators to draw a crowd. I told him about our trouble with brownies, and suggested he might charge out and throw a hammerlock on our friend if he showed up that night. We all had a big laugh over that idea.

The next day Jess and I fixed up the old smokehouse which Walker had built, then took his salmon out of the hold and washed them. We headed and split the backbones out of them, then soaked the sides overnight in a light brine. The next morning we spread the salmon

Murder Cove

sides on the racks of the smokehouse, cut a big pile of green alder, and started a fire beneath the racks. There are two ways of smoking fish: you can hard-smoke it by keeping a low fire going for several days, or you can kipper it in one long day with a slightly hotter fire. Jess and I planned to kipper it, then can it. This is a good method, since the fish keeps indefinitely.

We worked all day cutting alder and keeping the fire just right. At sunset we were still at it. I had told the women to hold supper so that we could finish.

Suddenly I heard Barb's scream from up toward the house. Then came Fink's frantic barking. My first thought was that the brownie had one of the boys. I had no rifle with me. Grabbing the axe, I ran up the dark trail toward the house. Brush broke ahead of me, then the dark shape of a bear was upon me. I jumped to the side of the trail and swung the axe with all my strength. I felt the blade graze him; then he was gone and Fink swept by barking hysterically. I ran on up the trail with the terrible fear that the bear had killed Barb or one of the boys.

In front of the house I met Barb with a flashlight. "The boys?" I gasped.

"They're inside," she said. "I was coming back from the well with a bucket of water and ran into him on the trail. Fink went right for him and he turned and ran down your way. I yelled a warning because I was afraid he might run into you and Jess."

"Jess!" I said, and ran into the house for my .30–06. A moment later I was back, took the flashlight from Barb, and ran down the trail.

I met Jess coming up. "Anybody hurt?" he asked.

"No—just scared. You see the bear?"

"See him! He damn near ran over the top of me!"

We walked back to the smokehouse where Fink stood barking. I was wet with sweat and trembling all over.

Back at the house I began to hurrah Jess. "Why didn't you grab the bear and hold him until I could get there with the axe—shouldn't bother an old bear wrestler like you."

"I won't wrestle an uneducated bear like that," Jess said disdainfully.

The next morning, while the women canned the smoked salmon, Jess and I vowed to get the brownie. We had saved the salmon heads, and now we put them in a burlap sack and left the sack on an open stretch of beach about 150 yards from the old cookhouse. We propped open a window that gave us a good view of the bait, set up a shooting bench, and took turns watching.

All day long we waited. Sea gull and eagles and ravens soon discovered the sack of salmon heads and began pecking at it—but no bear. Just before dark, as Jess and I smoked and talked quietly, the cries of the birds changed tone. We put out our cigarettes and picked up our rifles. The birds took to the air, and soon we saw the dark outline of a bear lumber up to the sack and sniff.

"Take him," I whispered to Jess.

Click went the safety. Jess steadied a moment, let his breath out gently—squeezed the trigger. *Blam!*

The bear dropped instantly.

"Where did you hold?" I asked

"Just ahead of his shoulder."

The bear had been quartering toward us. "Must have broken his neck," I said. "Put another into him."

Jess shot again, and we went down the beach, taking

Murder Cove

our time before going right up to him. He was dead; Jess's first shot had broken his spinal column just ahead of his hump.

"Look here!" Jess said, pointing to a long, shallow gash on one shoulder. "You *did* hit him with that axe!"

"I hope that's the last of the bears!" Barb said that night. But it didn't work out that way; the worst was yet to come, and the fickle finger of fate again pointed to Duke. . . .

18

Bear, Behind You!

A few days after the Padons left, Duke and Dutch came into Murder Cove on the *Salty* to deer hunt. The following day Dutch hunted the high ridge behind the cove, and Duke and I decided to run Bartlett Point late that afternoon. Sometimes the deer came down from the higher ground onto these heavily wooded points in the fall.

Before taking off with the skiff and outboard motor, Duke and I flipped a coin to see who "played dog." I was the dog. Duke would wait on the far side of the sand spit, while I went through the wooded point and drove the deer past him.

As we approached Bartlett Point we saw a three-year-old brownie on the beach turning over drift logs to get the sand fleas underneath. There is always something pathetic about seeing so large an animal reduced to this manner of feeding. I beached the skiff one hundred yards

Bear, Behind You!

from the bear to let Duke off, and as we watched, a trick of the breeze took our scent to the observing bear. He huffed loudly, then broke into the loose-jointed gallop that is characteristic of these animals, and crossed the sand spit onto the point itself.

"You watch that bear real close, Wayne!" Duke said. He threw a cartridge into the chamber of his .257 Roberts, flipped on the safety and started down the beach. "Watch that bear," he cautioned again.

"I'll cuff a runt like that alongside the head," I joked, and pushed the skiff out into deeper water with an oar. I started the motor and went along the beach, paralleling the path the bear had taken. A few minutes later I beached the skiff in a small bight on the far side of the spit and tied it to a drift log that was above the high-tide mark. I lifted out my .30–06, checked the loads, then looked back across the spit at Duke, some two hundred yards away: he was standing behind the five-foot log that had been one of our favorite deer stands since we first came to Alaska. Duke had killed his first buck from that same spot almost fifteen years before.

I turned and moved into the woods, with its deadfalls and heavy brush. I took it slow and easy, for the small brownie was out there somewhere, and you do not live to be an old-timer in this country without remembering the close calls of the past and trying to avoid them in the future. I didn't expect trouble from the bear, but I knew he was here, and I'd be ready for him.

As I moved into the woods I began to see fresh deer sign. The breeze was out of the southeast, just right. I came to the extreme tip of the point and started back through, knowing my scent would force any deer there to make a break across the spit to the protection of the large peninsula beyond. I regretted my luck of the flip of the coin; I could just picture Duke having his pick of several deer as they broke out into the opening.

A shot broke the stillness. I stopped, waiting. Another shot... then silence. Had Duke knocked down one, or two? Or had I run the bear onto him? I began to move again, then stopped abruptly as a dead limb cracked somewhere to my right. A buck, head down, was sneaking past me through the brush some forty yards away. He did not appear to have seen me. I stepped quickly behind a tree and slipped off my safety. He stopped suddenly, his head up; the evening sun through the trees touched the antlers. As he began to wheel, I whistled sharply to stop him—then shot. The buck's legs buckled beneath him.

I retrieved the brass from my chamber, put in a fresh cartridge, and made my way to where he lay. Puting the rifle down, I took out my knife and cut his throat, then skinned off the scent pads and began to dress him.

I was almost done when a noise in the brush caught my attention; a moment later the breeze brought a heavy, musky scent to my nostrils. Bear! I reached for my rifle and slipped the safety off. Presently the bear came into sight, the same small one we'd seen earlier. As I watched, it stopped and sniffed the air, head up. It had scented the blood of the deer. I picked up a small dead limb and rapped it sharply against the butt of my rifle. The bear peered near-sightedly in my direction for a brief moment, then wheeled suddenly and disappeared into the brush.

I went ahead with my dressing; when I had finished I made the buck into a pack and wriggled into the shoulder straps. Then, picking up my rifle, I headed back to the

Bear, Behind You!

spot where I'd left the skiff. I dropped the buck into the bow and looked across the water toward the big log. Duke was bending over the brown mound of a deer and off to his left I saw another. I untied the skiff rope and pushed out into the deep water before starting the outboard motor.

At the sound Duke stood up and looked toward me; he held both arms wide, then with fingers apart he put his thumbs to his temples to indicate big ones. He held up two fingers. I waved back, and Duke went on dressing.

This was the best time of the day. In a few minutes the sun would be gone. I lit a cigar and buttoned my wool shirt against the coming chill. I was daydreaming, pleased at our luck today, when I caught a sudden movement from the corner of my eye.

A brownie—not the small one, but a big bruiser—was out of the woods and moving across the sand spit in a hard lunging run. Duke, directly in his path, was still bent over his deer, unaware of the danger. "Bear! Behind you!" I shouted at the top of my lungs, and shut off the outboard motor.

Duke wheeled and saw his situation at a glance; by this time the bear was only a little over fifty yards away, moving straight for him. Duke said later, "I knew I had a mean bear on my hands as soon as I saw the sonofagun." He grabbed his rifle and brought it up in one smooth motion, steadied a brief moment, then shot.

I heard the report, but the brownie didn't even break stride. How could a fine, steady shot like Duke miss at that distance? He shot twice more at perhaps thirty yards, but still the bear didn't go down. *What was wrong?* I slipped a cartridge into the chamber of my rifle. I was beginning to worry now. Had Duke knocked off his scope somehow? The skiff was rocking gently in the swell, and my front sight was all over the place. I waited; surely Duke would put him down!

After his third shot Duke wheeled and ran to the far end of the big log. The brownie made the other end in one gigantic leap, and it was halfway down the log when Duke shot this time at perhaps ten feet. Then the bear was onto him, knocking him backward toward the water. They were so close now I couldn't tell what was happening. I saw Duke stumbling back into the bay, his rifle raised like a club. When he was waist-deep he made his stand.

I tried to hold a bead on the bear, but the motion of the skiff moved my front sight from the bear to Duke's broad back, then to the bear again. Indecision held me immobile. I was afraid to shoot—and afraid not to.

It is amazing what instinct does for a man in such a position. Duke said later, "I don't remember thinking about it, but my rifle was empty, and I had retreated just about as far as I was able; his mouth was open, and I knew he'd have me in a moment. I took the rifle by the barrel and hit the booger as hard as I could."

From the skiff I saw Duke hit him, then slip and fall. If I was to have my break, this must be it. For one brief second my wavering front sight settled on the bear's massive chest, and I shot a foot over Duke's back.

It was a good shot, for I could see the brownie slump, then right himself. Duke had somehow eased a couple of feet to one side, and I did not worry about hitting him so much; I began to shoot in earnest now. On the third

Bear, Behind You!

shot I knew I had him. He faltered, turned away from Duke, and then crawled laboriously back out of the water. I kept shooting, trying to break him down in the back. When my rifle was empty, I reloaded and then shot twice more into the motionless hulk on the beach. I held my fire, waiting. The huge head moved a couple of times, then sagged. I started up the outboard motor and ran the skiff ashore. Duke, soaking wet and white-faced, came down the beach to meet me, the broken rifle in his hands. Together we walked over to where the brownie lay, and I put the muzzle of my rifle against his ear and pulled the trigger. It was all over.

We stood silent and looked down at the bear. Streams of blood poured from a dozen holes in the dark hide.

"My cigarettes are all wet," Duke said at last.

I reloaded and leaned my rifle against the blood-spattered log. I fumbled in my shirt pocket, found one last cigar and cut it in half. We lit up. "I thought you were missing," I said.

Duke shook his head. "I think I hit him every time—I just couldn't put him down. I only had four cartridges in my rifle after I killed the two deer . . . I couldn't hold on his head that first shot when he was lunging across the spit, so I just shot at bear . . ."

Duke was shivering in his wet clothing, and we were both silent. In time the newness would wear off and it would be another close one to tell about, but now every little detail was etched in our minds.

"You hurt?" I asked.

"I don't think so."

I looked him over; sometimes a man can be hurt and not realize it, but he wasn't so much as scratched.

Duke began to strip and wring out his sodden clothing, then put it back on. "You know, I had forgotten all about you . . . then, after I hit him, *bam,* your bullet took him in the chest . . ."

"I was afraid of hitting you," I said. "I had to shoot right over you."

Duke looked at his rifle; the scope was smashed and the stock split. "Sure played hell with that."

We walked over to the bear. It was a big boar, weighing perhaps eight hundred pounds. We parted the long, dark-brown hair and located some of our shots. It was a job for the two of us to roll him over. One bullet had caught him high in the neck, angling back toward his heart; five more bullets had taken him in the chest, and one had smashed the right shoulder bone a foot below the socket. In all we counted seventeen bullet holes in the hide; two of my shots appeared to have gone completely through him. We would know more about it when we skinned him.

It was almost dark now. We began loading Duke's two bucks into the skiff, deciding to come back in the morning with Dutch to skin out the bear. We climbed in and I pushed the skiff out into deep water with an oar. I started the motor and headed toward home.

Suddenly my free hand began to shake uncontrollably—and it was not from the cold. My thoughts went back to that frightening moment of my first shot, when I had waited to see if I had hit the bear—or Duke. Perhaps he was thinking of it too, for he turned and grinned at me.

I looked back to the dark sand spit, then to the ragged outline of the mountains beyond, and I felt that special

Bear, Behind You!

kind of pride which comes rarely in a man's life when fate abruptly throws him into a dangerous, impossible situation—then leaves him to his own devices. I had shot on instinct alone, and never had I shot more coolly or accurately than I had today; never had I needed to.

19

The Lonely Land

With my brothers' departure I began to take care of the deer we had hanging in the meat house. Farther north, there is no problem keeping meat in the winter; residents of the interior butcher their moose and hang it up in a cache or meat house where animals can't get at it—and the below-freezing weather takes care of it once winter has set in. In the Alaskan panhandle it is different. There are two dominant weather conditions: a north wind clears the skies and sends the temperature down below freezing; southeasterly winds usually mean warmer weather and rain or snow. Consequently, if the wind is northerly there is cold weather and the meat is frozen solid; however, overnight the weather can switch to southeasterly, and the meat will begin to thaw. For this reason the meat must be preserved in some manner if a freezer is not available.

The Lonely Land

To preserve the deer, I had brought several large kegs and crocks over with us. Now I began sugar-curing venison hams and loins, which I would hang in the smokehouse over a low green alderwood fire after they had been cured. Some of the front quarters and loins I would corn in crocks.

I soaked the chunks of meat overnight to bring out the blood, washed them thoroughly, then put the meat in a salt and brown-sugar solution, with a little saltpeter to retain the rich red color of the meat. It would keep indefinitely this way. To use this meat, we would soak a chunk overnight in fresh water and it was ready to be cooked.

All of the meat scraps were ground into hamburger, and Barb seasoned it and made chili or spaghetti sauce, then canned it. She also canned venison roast with gravy, as well as small loin chops.

I had ordered pork side meat from town on the mailboat which I ground and mixed with ground venison, then seasoned it, using Pap's sausage recipe. We made it into patties, browned them in a skillet, then packed them into a crock and covered the patties with melted lard. They keep a long time this way.

Canadian honkers, mallards and teal filled the lagoon behind the house and the grass flats at the head of Murder Cove. We always had a dozen or more hanging in the meat house. When we had enough of them, I would fillet out the breasts and legs and Barb canned them.

I had made a crab pot and set it out in the bay. Whenever we wanted some Dungeness crabs, I would row out in the skiff and pull it. Sometimes there would be thirty or forty big male crabs in the pot. I would take as many as we would need, then turn the rest loose and rebait the pot.

Out near the entrance to the cove was a sandy clam beach. On every minus tide (usually occurring twice a month) we would all go out to the bed and dig a sack of clams. We would eat some fresh, either fried in batter or steamed, and the rest would be minced and canned to be used in chowder.

By the middle of November, when the bucks' necks began to swell with the coming mating season, we had all of our venison put up; it gave us a good feeling to see the shelves filled with cans of meat, fish and berries.

With our winter provisions taken care of, I turned to the cannery and began dismantling. It sometimes took all of my will power to stay with the work, for flocks of ducks and geese were passing low overhead as they moved back and forth from the back lagoon to the grass flats. This was a hunter's paradise, and at times I would put down my tools and look at Fink.

"What do you say, partner, should we go get them?"

Fink would jump up and down, wagging his tail and barking. We'd go to the house to get the shotgun and Mark; then all three of us would spend hours in the high grass of the flats, flushing small bunches of ducks from pot holes, or sneaking up on a flock of geese. Usually we would come home wet to the waist and chilled, but with a big string of birds. It was wonderful, and it was all ours.

Since Duke's ordeal at Bartlett Point we hadn't been bothered by brownies. We sometimes saw them on the beach across the bay, but not around the house. The cold north winds began in November, and they disappeared

The Lonely Land

into their private hibernation caves for the rest of the winter.

The days were getting much shorter now, and soon the winter snows began. We awoke each morning to a dazzling world of white. Barb and I would sit at the kitchen windows sipping our coffee and watch the wildlife which forever put on a show for us. Sometimes the gulls stood on a rock out in the bay and squawked over their pecking rights. Sometimes we watched a raven working to open a mussel shell he had found at low tide. The raven would fly into the air and drop the mussel onto the rocky beach. If the shell didn't crack the first time, the raven would repeat his bombing performance until it did, then eat it. On occasion we saw a mink come along the beach with a sea urchin in its mouth. What we enjoyed most were the land otters which cavorted and played on the end of a log that jutted out into the bay. Sometimes there would be seven or eight of them playing tag, sliding games or feeding at one time. Life was easy for them, for all they had to do was dive down to the bottom and catch small fish or crabs.

Almost every morning deer walked along the beach, perhaps sensing that they were safe from us now. There were gentle, soft-eyed does, and gaunt, rawboned bucks which had lost their antlers. These bucks were different animals now, worn out from fighting over the does, and without the fire of such a short time ago.

With the winter storms upon us, weeks went by when we didn't see anyone except Walt Sperl, who operated the mailboat, *Yakobi*, and dropped off our mail once a week if the weather permitted. Many people would have hated such isolation, but we enjoyed it.

— *THIS RAW LAND* —

In a way such a life is most desirable, for one is relieved of all the problems of society. *Time* might inform us that there is hate and violence over segregation issues in Georgia; that eight people died and many were hospitalized in Los Angeles because of the deadly smog; that 212 persons were killed in automobile accidents over Thanksgiving, or that a sex deviate had brutally murdered a small child in a Chicago suburb. We are concerned over these tragedies—but they hold no threat for us. Our problems are primeval in comparison. We are primarily concerned about brown bear wandering into our yard and killing our children, or having enough food put up to last us until spring.

We have no set hours, no social demands. Murder Cove is all ours; we may do as we please. I can stand and watch the exquisite shades of sunset behind the icy mountain mass to the west and let out a long, quavering wolf howl just so I may listen to the rock face of the cliff beyond the cove throw back the sound—and I will not be captured and deported to the funny farm or even censored for disturbing the peace.

Barb has her housework to keep her busy. With no electricity, she washes clothes by hand and does her chores without man-made conveniences. She is beginning to teach Mark to learn numbers and to read in preparation for the first grade next year.

Both Barb and I are voracious readers and we subscribe to various magazines and book clubs. Every mailboat brings literature of some kind. Sometimes if the weather is very stormy, it might be two or three weeks until the mailboat arrives, but what a joy it is to have a sack of letters, magazines and books to go through!

20

Dangerous Dan Willis

One stormy evening when big, white combers were rolling out in the strait, we saw a small outboard skiff coming into the bay.

"There's only one person I know of who would be running around in a skiff in this weather," I said to Barb. "It must be Dangerous Dan," and I went down to the dock to meet him.

Dangerous Dan Willis was an Indian who lived near Kake, on Kupreanof Island. He was a short, stocky man with the dark-brown hair and eyes of the Thlinget. His weathered brown face was friendly and he smiled often. Dan was between sixty-five and seventy years of age. He had gotten his nickname not because he was such a dangerous character, but because he sallied forth on his trapping and seal-hunting trips in all kinds of weather.

"How . . . white man!" Dan said, holding up a palm

in peace as he imitated some of the Indians he'd seen in movies.

"Hello, Dan," I said, "you keep running around in this kind of weather, and the otter people will get you." Most Thlingets believe in the *kustakaw* (their boogeyman), who took the form of an otter and lured people away and changed them into otters.

"Ho! Ho! Ol' Dangerous Dan wise to otter people—they never git him!"

We shook hands and I saw that Dan had eight or nine seal carcasses in his skiff.

"By golly, I sure like to stay two-tree day," Dangerous Dan said. "Take care of seals."

On the beach was a row of small red shacks in which the Indian families had lived when the cannery had operated. I pointed to the first one. "That end cabin has a wood-burning stove, Dan," I said. "You're welcome to move in and stay as long as you like."

Dan had known of this shack with the stove, for he had used it regularly when Walker had been here. In fact on his last stay, he had left a supply of wood stacked neatly on the porch. Dan was pleased that I had made the offer, for that was what he had wanted in the first place. "By golly, maybe I do that," he said.

"I'll go tell Barb you'll have supper with us, Dan."

Dan looked troubled. "Ol' Dangerous Dan kinda smell like ol' bull seal," he said, worried about what Barb would think.

"Don't worry about it, Dan," I said, and started back up the dock.

Dan untied his little cabin skiff and started the outboard motor. He beached the skiff on the sandy beach in

Dangerous Dan Willis

front of the cabin, and pulling up the tops of his hip boots, carried his camping equipment ashore.

I told Barb to count on Dan for supper; then the boys and Fink went with me down the trail toward Dan's shack.

Dan had a fire going and was melting snow in a big pan on the back of the stove. He had carried in his sleeping bag and provisions. When everything was shipshape, he rolled the seal carcasses out of his skiff and floated them ashore. Now he prepared to dress them. First he picked up a rock on the beach, showed it to the boys, then used it as a whetstone to sharpen the short, curved blade of his skinning knife. I had watched Indians do this before—it always seemed to me they picked up the first rock they saw, but it had to be a special type of rock, or so Dan told the boys.

Dan, one of the last of the old-time seal hunters, hadn't succumbed to the dubious aid of the regular checks from the state or federal agencies as some of his fellow Indians had. He was intensely proud that he earned his own way instead of squandering away the little he made fishing in the summer and then living off welfare in the winter. In fact, when Dan had turned sixty-five, he had refused to apply for social security benefits, until finally a white man had convinced him it was not charity, but money due him which he had earned as a powder monkey years before.

Dangerous Dan gutted the seals, saving only the liver, and I helped him drag them up onto the porch of the shack. Tomorrow he would skin them. The scalps would be sent to the Fish and Game Department, which paid a bounty of three dollars for each of them. The skins would be fleshed, salted and shipped to a fur buyer. Dan would render out the blubber and store the rich seal oil in empty gallon wine jugs; many of the older Indians craved seal oil from the old days, and Dan received a good price in the village for it. Seal meat is extremely dark—almost black. Choice parts would be saved, including the flippers, which the Indians smoke and consider a delicacy.

When we finished dragging the seal carcasses up to the porch, Dan went down to the sea and washed his bloody hands, drying them on his wool trousers. He put a seal liver into a pan and walked back up to the house with us for supper.

After Barb greeted Dan, he handed her the pan, saying, "Seal liver for you, Missus Wayne."

"Thank you, Dan," Barb said, and took the liver into the kitchen to soak overnight in a pan of salt water.

When we had eaten we sat back and talked of current events, the past summer's fishing season, and the number of deer we had put up for the winter. I told Dan of the trouble we'd had with the brown bear.

"Brown bear bad!" Dan exclaimed, and began telling us bear stories.

Presently there came the *chirp, chirp* of an otter out on the beach in front of the house, and immediately Dan warned us to watch the boys very closely, as the otters would toll them away to their dens and change them into otter people. We agreed, knowing how strongly the older Thlingets believe the superstition.

I have never made fun of the Indian beliefs. We can scarcely censor them for believing in witches and otter people when our own history is filled with superstitions. It is not hard to understand how the Thlinget accepts these

Dangerous Dan Willis

beliefs: most of the Indians have heard them since early childhood.

I asked Dan if he had ever seen an otter man change form. Dan nodded; one time at Kake he'd seen a land otter run up the beach into the woods—a moment later a man had stepped out and walked down to the beach. Another time, years before this, Dan had met a strange Indian on Kuiu Island while he was hunting. Dan suspected he was one of the otter people, and as they talked, Dan refused to meet the stranger's eye—for the otter people could hypnotize humans and lead them away to their den. Finally Dan filled his pipe with tobacco, lit it, then offered it to the man. But it was refused. This proved that the stranger was of the otter people, for it was known they fear fire and smoke. To this day many natives who do not smoke carry cigarettes while hunting, and use these to test whether strangers they meet in the woods are otter people.

The next day, while Dangerous Dan skinned his seals and rendered out the seal oil, I took his empty .22 cases up to the house and reloaded them. For many years my brothers and I had reloaded all of our own ammunition, and we had dies for all the popular calibers. Dan was immensely pleased when I returned with the cartridges.

For several days he hunted around Carol Island and Surprise Harbor. Then one morning he loaded all his things aboard the little cabin cruiser and headed for the Indian village of Kake to sell his seal oil and meat, and to ship the scalps and hides.

This was the last we ever saw of this charming little man, for he challenged the persistent sea once too often

—and came out the loser. His people found part of his skiff off the Keku Islands, but for Dangerous Dan himself—it was felt the otter people had at last found him in a weakened condition and claimed him for one of their own.

21

The Changing Land

January and February are the doldrums for the resident of the brush. Christmas and New Year holidays have gone, snow banks become higher and higher, and it seems your whole world consists of cutting wood for the heater, shoveling snow, carrying endless buckets of water, eating and sleeping. Radio commercials are urging you to drop everything and take a sun break in Mexico City or Hawaii —and here you sit trapped, ten million miles from anywhere!

In February the snow really began to pile up, and the deer began to starve in great numbers. Driven out of the woods onto the beaches they ate kelp at low water and nibbled at dead limbs; the bucks and last year's fawns were the worst off. One could not walk a hundred yards without seeing a deer carcass. The does, with new fawns inside of them, seemed to carry a reserve of fat to hold them over the hard times, until the snow melted and the first buds came to the brush.

I took the chain saw and began felling yellow cedar trees along the edge of the woods for them to feed upon. This saved a great many deer, but we worried to think of the hundreds dying elsewhere that we could do nothing for. The Fish and Game men state that this is good in areas where there are no wolves or many hunters to keep the deer from over-populating. Perhaps they are right, but still it is pitiful to watch the poor creatures starving.

As I felled trees I sometimes found deer so weak they could not get to their feet. There was nothing I could do for the gaunt bucks, but the last spring's fawns I usually carried home. I put them in our former meat house, and the boys and Barb fed them scraps of bread and oatmeal. I cut armloads of cedar branches for them to eat, and we saved many of them. Sometimes we had fifteen or twenty in the meat house at a time. Often the fawns, like any other animals, differed in looks and temperament; soon we were able to tell them apart, and began to name them. One with extremely long ears became Rabbit, others Pauncho, Socks, Pasquamie, Glutton, Dude, Mary Ann, Helen, Candance, and so on. As they became stronger they would follow the boys and Barb around, and try to come right into the house. In the mornings several of them would be pawing on the back door, letting us know they were hungry.

The days slipped by and suddenly we began to notice how much longer they were than a month before. Now it was March, and there was a definite feeling of spring not too far away.

The Changing Land

In late March a warm southeasterly wind and rain cut the snow, and buds popped out almost overnight on the brush. One by one our fawns drifted away until the meat house was empty. For several weeks some of them would occasionally turn up at the back door to say hello and accept a crust of bread before disappearing into the woods again.

During the first sunny days of April we began to see our brown-bear neighbors again as they came out of hibernation. They patrolled the beaches, eating little at first, until their shrunken stomachs expanded. Their food now was skunk cabbage roots, carcasses of winter-killed deer, and the tender shoots of grass. Quite often we would see a huge female with from one to three small cubs. The cubs, born in the dens, weigh only one and a half pounds or so at birth. Even when they are seen with their mother in early spring they seem absurdly small. Later on they grow at a fantastic rate.

Most naturalists agree that the female brown or grizzly bear gives birth every three years. On numerous occasions I have observed a female with large two-year-old cubs. These bears are not gregarious, and about the only time you see more than one traveling together is during mating season, or when a mother is with her cubs.

One day I saw a large female with two small cubs across the bay, and as I watched them with the binoculars I spotted what appeared to be a three-year-old bear following them at a discrete distance. When they stopped to feed on some tender new grass shoots, the fourth bear slowly eased up to join them. As he drew near, the big female charged and bit him on the shoulder and drove him into the woods. Even from my distance I could hear his cry of pain and despair. He was her previous cub, but now that she was with her new little ones she wanted nothing to do with him.

If a person spends a good part of his time living and hunting and trapping certain areas, he learns a great deal about the wildlife of that particular part of the country. Over the years he becomes acquainted with certain bears. The big sow that I just mentioned was one I had known for several years. In fact, I had seen her two years before with the big cub she was now chasing away. It was just a matter of putting all of the pieces of the puzzle together.

The mother went back to the small cubs, licked them, and continued along the beach. Presently the big cub limped out of the woods and again began following them. He kept his distance for a while, sometimes sitting on his haunches like a big dog as he watched the trio ahead. He was a picture of utter despair—the abandoned teen-ager with head and feet much too big for the rest of him. A half hour later he had crept within twenty yards of them, and the enraged mother wheeled abruptly and ran him off again. A little later back he came, perhaps with the idea that if he persisted, his mother would relent and let him join the family.

For the next several days I saw them, the pathetic outcast always in the background. A short time ago, the mother had been ready to fight to the death for him; now she no longer cared. His place had been taken by the little ones.

When I saw them again a week or so later, the big cub was no longer in evidence. Very likely, after all the rebuffs, he had finally gotten the message and gone off on his own.

The Changing Land

Early one morning, as I sat at the kitchen table having coffee and watching the delicate shades of orange coloring the eastern sky, I saw the dark shape of a bear moving across the tide flats back of the house. The animal was perhaps two hundred yards away, moving slowly as it grazed along on the new shoots of salt-water grass. It was an extremely large bear, and there was something vaguely familiar about it. I went into the front room, picked up the binoculars and focused them upon the animal. Now I was sure; it was Big Brownie!

My brothers and I had known the big fellow for nearly ten years. It had been three years since I'd last seen him, and I had thought perhaps he had died of old age.

Since World War II it has been fashionable for the world's big-game hunters to have a good-sized brown bear in their trophy rooms. Consequently the ranks of the really large brownies have shrunk considerably. Today an Admiralty Island brownie whose hide squares nine feet is considered a *big* bear.

Big Brownie was the largest brown bear I had ever seen. On several occasions in the past I had crept within a hundred yards of him and studied him with the glasses. At times he reminded me of a huge, shaggy draft horse, and I knew there were men who would pay thousands of dollars for the chance to collect his hide. All of the local big-game guides who brought spring and fall bear-hunting parties into the area knew him. He had escaped these hunters' guns for several reasons: he was smart and extremely difficult to stalk, and he began to "rub" unusually early in the spring, so even if a hunter had the luck to get within range—his coat was badly rubbed and worthless.

— *THIS RAW LAND* —

Now, just out of hibernation, his long, dark-brown winter coat glistened. He was truly something to behold. I awoke Barb and the boys and brought them into the kitchen to see this rare creature, for he must be terribly old, and this might be the last time we'd see him.

We watched him graze across the grass flats toward the peninsula, and half an hour later he disappeared into the woods.

After breakfast I picked up my rifle and the boys and I went out and followed his tracks. I knew that somewhere I would find a clear set of prints in the clay soil, and I had the yardstick to measure them. Presently we found clear tracks, and I knelt down with the yardstick and checked a hind footprint. It measured a whopping seventeen inches long, and I found I could put both of my boots side by side into the print without covering either side! He was some bear! I guessed his hide would have squared twelve feet, but I fervently hoped the bear hunters would never get the chance to measure it. . . .

For days flocks of ducks and geese passed overhead on their way north for the summer. Canadian honkers, as usual, flew high in enormous V-shapes, their lonesome cries invading the spirit, making a man want to drop everything and join the migration. Sometimes we saw long strings of swans, great wings outstretched as they beat their way northward.

The warm days continued, and where there had been snow not long before, there was now foot-high grass. Blueberry, huckleberry and salmonberry brush was fully leaved, and as the sun warmed the tops of the tall spruce trees we listened to the continuous booming as male

The Changing Land

grouse puffed their throats and sent out mating calls. Schools of herring, and even a whale or two, began to show in the bay. All of this made us realize we must soon move back to Warm Springs Bay, for it would be time for me to go fishing once more.

I began to build a log float, on which I planned to load my share of the lumber I had salvaged during the winter. We would then wait for a calm day and tow it home.

One day in mid-May Dutch arrived on the *Salty* to give us a hand. He and I spent the following two days loading lumber aboard the raft and then lashed it all down. Then we began packing our personal gear and loading it aboard the boats. Now it was just a matter of waiting for a dead-calm day to make the crossing.

One evening when Dutch and I were sitting on the porch soaking up the last rays of the dying sun and waiting for Barb's call to supper, we spotted Big Brownie ambling along the far shore of the bay. Even at the distance he was impressive. We both watched the great beast in silence until at last he disappeared around a little point.

"You know," Dutch said at last, "this country is changing, Wayne. I was over grouse hunting in Chapin Bay not long ago and there's a logging outfit making a hell of a mess of the mountainside. There's one in Eliza Harbor, too, and another big outfit due to begin operations in Whitewater Bay." Dutch rolled a cigarette and lit it with a swipe of a match along his thigh. "Got statehood now. Gonna see a lot of changes in this country. Governor's promising three big state ferries and a marine highway system that will link Prince Rupert to all the major towns in southeastern Alaska and connect up with the Haines Cutoff to the north." The sun was gone now, and there was a chill to the evening air. A morose look was on Dutch's face. "First thing you know, tourists will be looking over our shoulders asking silly questions and snapping pictures of everything that moves—if there's any wildlife left by then . . ."

I nodded. We were all misfits, or we wouldn't be living our lives out in this violent, isolated land. Duke and I could accept the change, even if we disliked it, but Dutch was different. He reminded me of the old "Mountain Men" of the West when the buffalo and beaver were all gone and there was no place for them as towns and cities were founded and industry began to spring up.

Barb's call to supper brought us to our feet, but I was still troubled by my thoughts. On a hill beyond the house a grouse boomed, and from the bay there came the chirp of an otter.

The next evening we had a favorable weather forecast; the barometer was holding steady, so at two o'clock the following morning we rose and carried the last of our things onto the boats. By three we had our tow lines connected to the raft, and with the *Salty* pulling ahead, we caught the ebb tide out of Murder Cove and began to cross the strait.

Behind us was the darkened outline of the dock; beyond, the aurora borealis colored the northern sky with an ever-changing pattern of magic. On the back deck Barb and the boys stood watching in fascination. Presently they stepped into the wheelhouse. "In a way I hate to leave Murder Cove," Barb said.

I nodded, knowing exactly how she felt. Dutch had

The Changing Land

been right last night: the vanguards of civilization—the encroaching logging operations and accompanying pulp mills—were already making a change on this virgin island, and our wilderness boundaries would soon be cut down a little more. In the years to come we would see a great many more changes as the rapidly expanding outside world needed more and more raw materials. In time, it would be the story of the West all over again.

From out of the darkness there came the lonely cry of a loon. Perhaps it was just my mood as I thought back to my talk with Dutch, but there seemed to be a note of anguish in the bird's long, quavering cry. Could it be, I wondered, that like my brothers and me, this dweller of lonely, isolated spots instinctively knew his days were numbered?

Adventures of a modern family which moved to the last Frontier on an isolated Alaskan island shortly after World War II.

Wayne Short tells what Alaska was like as a pioneer a half-century ago in his books:
The Cheechakoes
This Raw Land
Albie, and Billy, the Sky Pilot & other stories

Author Wayne Short is the great nephew of Luke Short, buffalo hunter, army scout, gambler and friend of Wyatt Earp and Bat Masterson. Wayne tells the story of his life in *Luke Short, A Biography*.

~~~~~~~~~~~~~~~~~~~~~~~

____	*The Cheechakoes*	$15.95
____	*This Raw Land*	$15.95
____	*Albie, & Billy, etc.*	$13.95
____	*Luke Short, etc.*	*$14.95*

Enclose $2.00 for shipping (USPO)

Send check or money order to:

DEVIL'S THUMB PRESS
P.O.Box 704
Hereford, Arizona 85615
e-mail: devilsthumbpress@theriver.com